C H O R A L

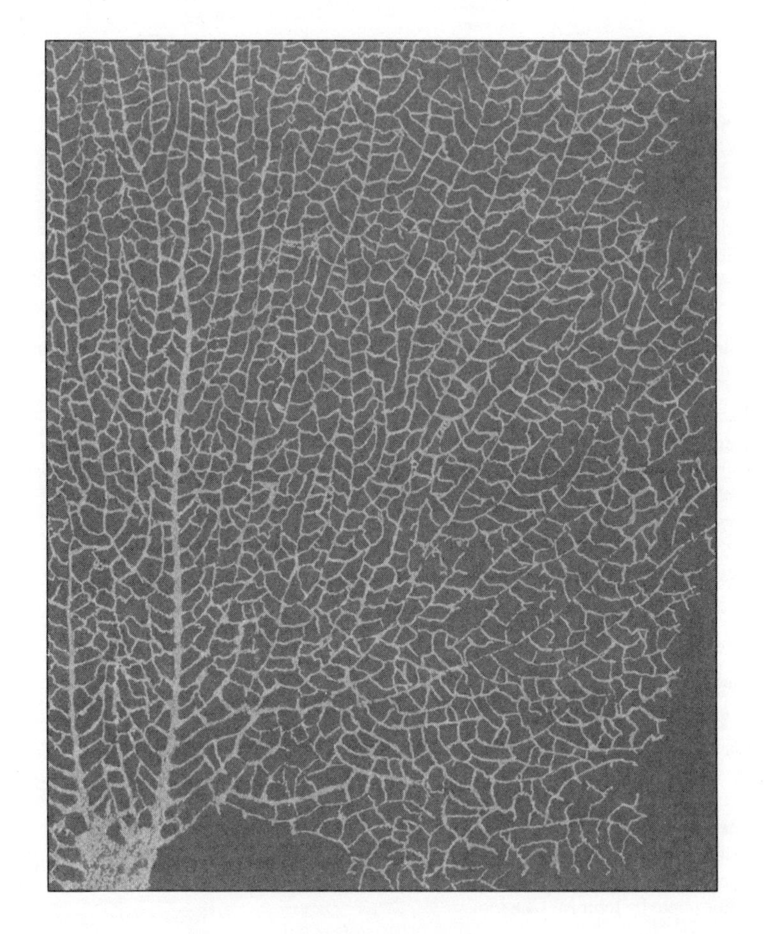

a novel

Karen McLaughlin

Press Gang Publishers / Vancouver

1 2 3 4 5 98 97 96 95

First edition 1995

The Publisher acknowledges financial assistance from the Canada Council, the Book Publishing Industry Development Program of the Department of Canadian Heritage, and the Cultural Services Branch, Province of British Columbia.

The author gratefully acknowledges the use of phrases from the following works by Julia Kristeva, all published in English translation by Columbia University Press, New York: *Desire in Language* (1980, translated by Thomas Gora, Alice Jardine and Leon S. Roudiez); *Revolution in Poetic Language* (1984, translated by Margaret Waller); and *Tales of Love* (1987, translated by Leon S. Roudiez).

CANADIAN CATALOGUING IN PUBLICATION DATA

McLaughlin, Karen, 1954–
Choral

ISBN 0-88974-045-3

1. Title
PS8575.L38C56 1995 C813'.54 C95-910353-8
PR9199.3.M34C56 1995

Edited by Nancy Pollak
Design by Val Speidel
Cover art © 1995 by Karen McLaughlin, *Heart*, oil pastel on paper
Author photo by John McLaughlin
Typeset in Electra
Printed and bound in Canada by Best Book Manufacturers
Printed on acid-free paper ♾

Press Gang Publishers
101 - 225 East 17th Avenue
Vancouver, B.C. V5V 1A6 Canada

for my mother
Cora
with love
and gratitude
for allowing me to use
her beautiful name
in this work of fiction

what is told through the experience of the body
is never forgotten

ACKNOWLEDGEMENTS

Heartfelt thanks to Reesa Brotherton who was always there to comfort me throught the writing of this novel; Pauline Butling for special encouragement; Mary Lou Riordon-Sello and Rob Milthorp for providing visual images; Marie-Andrée Laberge for a frank reading of the first draft; Mary Ann Cherney, Joan Caplan, Suzanne Sarioglu, Linda Anderson Stewart, Dianne Swanson and Sandra Vida for nurturing friendship and laughter; the Creative Writing Program at the University of Calgary, particularly Aritha van Herk, Fred Wah, Roberta Rees and the fellow-writers of English 496, 92/93; Alberta College of Art for its stimulating atmosphere; *Absinthe* and the Crowsnest Pass Workshop and Retreat; Franklyn Heisler, former curator of the Muttart Art Gallery, Calgary, for providing the space that began *Choral*; EM/ Media, Calgary, where I learned about video-making and its structures.

Special thanks to Nancy Pollak, my editor, and to Val Speidel for her care and attention in the design of this book, and to Barbara Kuhne and Della McCreary at Press Gang Publishers for facilitating a smooth and pleasurable experience publishing this novel.

To Julia Kristeva, literary critic and psychoanalysist whose intellectual property I have used in fragmented phrases throughout *Choral*, a very special thanks.

To John McLaughlin and our daughters Sara Juel and Jennifer Morain, forever love and thanks for your support and encouragement.

CONTENTS

AS A PRESENCE THAT PRECEDES x

THE REVENANT 3

PUTTING AN END TO THEIR JUXTAPOSITION 6

my hands are still cold 11

EYEWITNESS FROM THE ALLEY 19

slice me up 21

THE TESTIMONY OF ROXY FRENCH 31

for an itchy monkey 35

LOQUACIOUS LILA 46

I never get out of bed 50

AN IDEALIZED MISCONCEPTION 58

THE REPOSITORY 61

the pleasure of you 64

MRS. JOSEPH FINALLY SPEAKS 72

the noise of my pain 75

THE REMNANT 81

THE TESTIMONY OF A STRANGER 83

SELVAGE 88

neither model nor copy 91

SET BACK IN RELATION TO 100

PATSY'S PRATTLE 104

A CERTAIN BALANCE BETWEEN THE TWO 107

my sorrow and rage 111

INTO HER IMPOSSIBILITY 116

the difference between pleasure and pain 119

THE COMPLICITY BETWEEN THEM 126

THE REMONSTRANT 128

AND SPLITS INTO 132

I lift from the slit of my life 134

THE REMANENCE 141

THE RENASCENT 144

WHO WILL SPEAK FOR MY SHORT LIFE 147

behind me and in front of me 149

OUT OF THE RETICULUM 155

AS A PRESENCE THAT PRECEDES

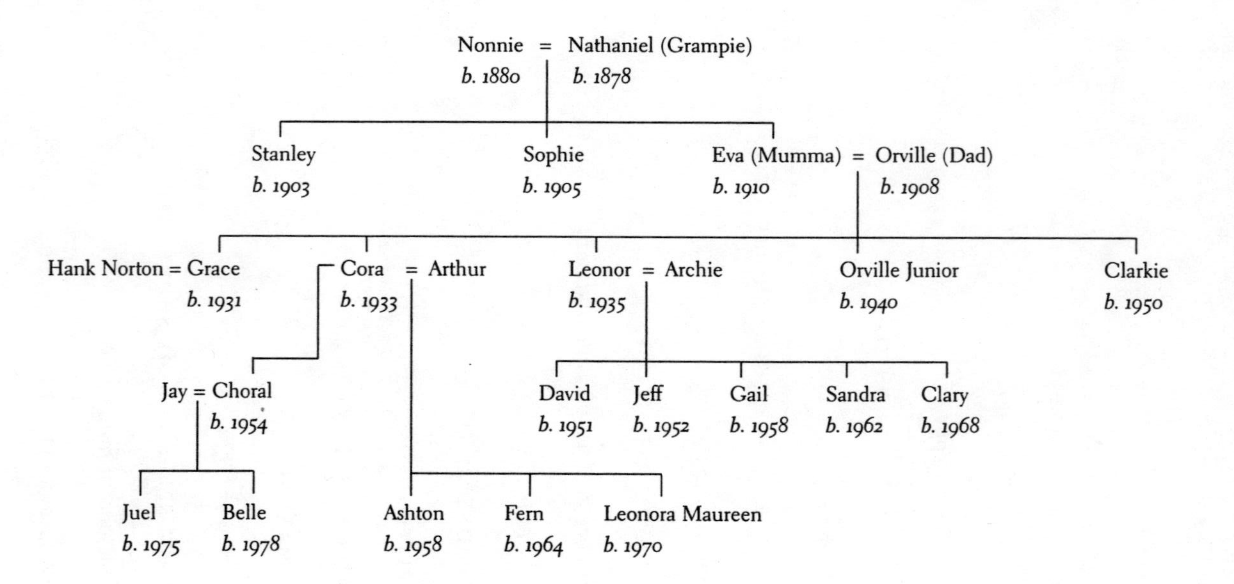

Friends and Familiars: Loretta Roxy French Lila Mrs. Joseph Patsy Sall Reowna

Choral

think of me as a woman

Mind you it's true enough, that story about me almost dying when I was thirteen. Of appendicitis. For a long time afterwards I ailed and wasted away on the horsehair couch, pale as a ghost they'd say. Or perhaps she saw a ghost. My old father Nathaniel would tolerate no such talk. Foolish mouths. Foolish mouths. Yis all has foolish opening mouths, he'd bark.

Well, I never opened my mouth.

And never did cry. Except when I rolled the taste of my own blood around my mouth. To disappear into your own body, there's nothing like the taste of a bloody mouth. I should have learned to fight back. I should have learned to spit blood. Spit red. Blood, opened and deepening, that peculiar red wine colour of betrayal that sinks when you let it cure. Dried blood.

I always glossed it over with a wet smacking kiss.

Oh well, I suppose it doesn't matter now.

But I'll tell you something not another living soul knows. Before I almost died, I saw a tall hard creature with beautiful hands whose fingers were cracked off right below the knuckles. Both hands. Imagine. Down she reached, silent as stone, with such a pose of peace and concern I almost reached back. I could have reached but I was stricken. Do you appear to cure or do you appear to sink, I wanted to screech but my mouth wouldn't open. Are your fingers broken or do they only appear to be broken, I screeched behind a skewered mouth. And the fury of my silent screech caused the peaceful creature to part her lips, to spew a speech of falling teeth that clinked to my feet. What an apparition. What a holy witch. An Ecum Secum witch.

I wanted to reach, reach for her, clasp her hands, but was so alarmed by those blunt cracked stubs staring at me and all those teeth falling at my feet, I just covered my face and held my breath.

Breathe my beauty. Breathe my beauty, the creature whispered to me.

So I breathed and breathed and old father bought me a pump organ. Poor Sophie was as mad as all-get-out, some sister she was. Since she was the oldest she always thought the father should favour her, and except for that one incident in our lives, he truly did. I let her use it when she wanted but she just couldn't stand the fact that it was mine. Eva's organ. In the end it made no difference 'cause I couldn't play it anyway. I just couldn't. Every time old father hollered at me to practise all I could see were my hands with their fingers cracked off at the knuckles. Where the missing fingers had gone to, I never could imagine. I was stupid and frightened that if my fingers stayed in those stiff practice positions too long, or got too cold and froze, they would snap off. Sometimes I even thought I could hear my missing fingertips clink to the hard ground. Clink. Clink like a song you thought you'd heard before.

Now, Orville, that son-of-a-bitch husband of mine, he could make a song and play the violin. Play it like a fiddle to make me dance or like a real violin to make me cry. Played by ear. Tight or sober, day or night. Not that he was a drinker, mind you. Had a few snorts now and then, but who doesn't. Besides old father, I mean. A drop of liquor never passed those mean lips, never sweetened that cranky mouth, that old white-haired man. Nathaniel the good. Oh yes, he was a real good man alright.

They were both good men. Nathaniel and Orville. Never let a woman lift anything heavier than a platter of potatoes. Though my mother Nonnie carried three babies, me being the youngest, and then I carried five. Anyway, the women were never required to do hard work, like carrying water or loads of wood. Even after we got married Orville used to hang all the clothes out on the line for me. But when he went away to the war, I was left alone with the burden of a house to keep clean and scrubbed and meals to cook for three little girls. The thought of it still leaves me stricken. All that fuss and mess with only a bawling baby boy for comfort during the long, long evenings.

Just before Dad went away to the war he got us all upstairs. Leonor, Grace, Junior and me. Just the four of us then, Clarkie wasn't born till years later. I was the last one rounded up and he started in on me first. Cora, Cora, he tut-tut-tutted, you're always the one to cause me trouble.

Down on the bed he sat us and then he launched into his big speech. I'm going away and I don't know when I'll be back, you have to be good to Mumma. You have to do this and you have to do that, he flew on with his great big yap. You have to be good to Eva. I knew what it was going to be like when he rounded us up, so I put a diaper pin in my pocket. You have to do this and you have to do that and when we'd had about enough of that blowhard, I drove the pin into Junior's arse.

All hell broke loose. Orville threw his arms up in the air blubbering and cursing. I can't talk to you kids, I can't do nothing with yis, he spat and then stomped out.

We couldn't stand it and poor little Junior had to pay.

He was a blowhard alright. A big bloody fraud and blowhard. And he loved himself. So vain was our daddy Orville. Knew for sure he was a real big handsome man. All around the house he'd be whistling and singing like Bing Crosby. Every time he'd pass a mirror he'd just have to stop and look at himself, wink his foolish wink and make out like he was going to play his violin. Oh he could play the fiddle like anything. But he was a flop. And he never knew it and neither did Mumma, poor silly woman, she was always, always crazy about him. Those two. Where did all that foolishness lead. They had no sense to rub between them.

When you think about the way we lived.

Before the war they were away all the time. I would sit for hours at night and rock Junior, listening to the radio. We ate apples. They'd make meals sometimes but nothing you'd ever want to eat. Maybe some burnt liver, old cold potatoes and a can of peas if they could be bothered. To tell the truth, I can never remember sitting down to a meal with them. Any meals were at weird times and always on trays.

Who the hell wants to eat all their meals on trays.

When they were home there was always a gang of Dad's family around. You were lucky to get near the table. One time I watched one of the aunts scrape the gunk off their plates, then load them up with fried bologna and grey mashed potatoes for us kids, not even rinsing the forks and knives. I almost threw up. So I told Dad and he gave me some money to get a hamburger, but warned me not to tell. He didn't have enough money left after a weekend of boozing to buy us all hamburgers. As long as they had enough money, they always gave us some when they couldn't be bothered to feed us. Money to go to the show or to the joint around the corner to eat junk.

Most of the time we didn't have much money and sometimes not enough to eat. We weren't even kept clean. Bedbugs and cockroaches and god-knows-what else. Mumma was useless around the house. Couldn't cook, didn't even hang the clothes out on the line. When he was around Dad did all that. And he was pretty well always around until the war. Then never again. He couldn't settle. Left the navy and worked on the boats, gone here and there for six months at a time. Mumma flew into rages and took her wrath out on us.

My little sister Leonor never got over it. Mumma was so hard on her, what a witch. One time she caught poor little Leonor getting something out of her bureau and went at her with a belt, beating her about the head and shoulders. Grace and I screeched and screeched but she turned and lashed at us. What a miserable old witch.

I never did figure out what Leonor was after.

Sometimes it was nice when Dad wasn't home but it was always hellish when he was. All they did was drink. Grace got the worst of it, but Grace could always look after herself and Leonor couldn't. That was the difference between them.

Grace, Grace, Grace, come down quick, Mumma screeched one afternoon. Dad was beating her, kicking her, ripping her blouse to shreds. Grace picked her up and as always, all Mumma could ever do was cry. But you know, they were both drunk and she never could fight back. Grace was twelve and I was going on eleven. That's the year I got so sick. He used to make me so mad.

One time we were all down in Ecum Secum at Nonnie and Grampie Nathaniel's, with Leonor and I sharing a mattress on the landing upstairs. Before they even had electricity and it was damned dark. Leonor cried that she wanted to go to bed with Grampie Nathaniel. Get to sleep, they hollered from downstairs but she kept on and on. What do you want to sleep with old Grampie Nathaniel for, I asked, all he does is fart and snore. Mumma and Aunt Sophie must have heard me 'cause they started to laugh and laugh. I suppose Dad wasn't getting any attention so up the stairs he came. When he bent down to give us a whack, I upped with my two feet and let him have it in the backside. He almost flipped over the rail. Mumma and Aunt Sophie went into hysterics and Dad couldn't get his breath. Now stop, now stop, he choked, but I told him to get his big arse out of there and leave us alone. When he realized they were laughing at him he turned on his high horse and muttered, oh that Cora, I don't know.

Too bad he hadn't gone over the rail.

After that great big fight in the afternoon, Grace dragged Mumma to the couch and held the shreds of her blouse to her mouth. Split open, Mumma's mouth was split wide open. She was always screeching at Grace to help her when they got into it. 'Cause she was the oldest, I guess.

Mumma called to me that she wanted some pop from the store but her purse was in the livingroom where Dad was clomping around. There he was, snorting and puffing like an old pig. Mumma's blood on his sweaty white shirt.

I was almost too scared to go in there so I picked up a broom and threatened to fight him if he ever came near me.

---

she didn't grieve about Mumma, Eva, her mother's
mother, skinny woman with poppy eyes, thigh roid
problems they say, can't figure out what legs have to
do with eyes but then she gets her legs cut off

my hands are still cold

so what can Choral really say when her mother Cora phones to ask   why didn't you send a wreath for Mumma's funeral   can't afford one Choral offers she doesn't send flowers and she is too far away to come to the funeral   (wonders if they use a short short coffin)   Eva didn't go to her own mother's funeral (legs bad by then) or to her youngest daughter's funeral (didn't walk by then) or even her oldest daughter's funeral (couldn't walk by then) either still   Choral wishes she had gone if only to see the faces of all the granddaughters who hadn't seen Eva for all those years   why did they go (how were they found)   when she is still alive in the nursing home Choral takes Eva an azalea plant blooming hugely pink   Eva doesn't like the woman in the bed next to her   all the noises and she shits herself   tells Choral I've been out to the clothesline this morning   my hands are still cold

what promise I held

but Eva drags Cora by her braids to her great-grandmother's funeral   (Choral thinks this must be Caroline Conrad   Nonnie's mother who came from Scotland so maybe it wasn't a great-great-great-grandmother who ran away with the gardener but just a great-great-grandmother)   Eva makes Cora kiss Caroline Conrad's cheek and her cheek is so waxy and smells so stinky Cora almost throws up

her mother's mother, skinny woman

I've been screeching since the day I was born and

the summer when Junior is born Cora is seven years old   Orville is home off the boat   taking care of the three little girls   after a few days he can't cope with Cora's long fine hair so he cuts off her braids at the nape of her neck   he cuts off her braids at the nape of her neck with the kitchen scissors   marches Cora upstairs braids in hand to the master bedroom to Eva and Junior   she keeps screeching when I brush her hair he rants   she's been screeching since the day she was born and she's still screeching

I'm still screeching

Cora is eight the first year she lives in Ecum Secum joins her sister Leonor   in bed they giggle draw pictures on each other's backs or scratch and rub   on the organ in the front room the music sheets are covered with pencil drawings of pretty girls in pretty dresses with flowing hair and blue pen eyes drawn by Cora and Leonor (and Grace when she comes in the summer)   they play the old pump organ too *up a lazy river how happy we will be*   when she grows up Choral wants to draw and play just like them but Cora says they're no good   the year in Ecum Secum is such a good year for Cora she has such a strong and clear voice she's picked to sing *Away in a Manger* all by herself at the Christmas concert   so when Choral is eight she wants to sing *Away in a Manger* all by herself   Cora sews her a red velvet dress full skirt trimmed with white rabbit fur   Choral is so scared   she can't sing loud enough

I am in love with Jimmy McNeil

the pump organ is Eva's a present when she is thirteen because she almost dies of appendicitis a present for living or almost dying Aunt Sophie says Eva was spoiled for life after that Sophie five years older than Eva leaves the farm in Ecum Secum gets a job in Shipton at the five-and-dime sends for Eva when her time comes they marry brothers big handsome fishermen who join the navy and sail away Eva never lets Aunt Sophie forget she was a virgin when she got married

can't figure out what legs have to do with

---

this fight in my chest

Cora is sick the year she is eleven   begs Eva to take
her to the doctor   severe anaemia he says doesn't
even know how this child is walking   when she is
wide awake in the middle of the day Cora sees
horrible monsters with open mouths but no sound
comes out   big horrible monsters slimy brown with
poppy eyes and missing teeth   fatten her up they
say   big horrible monsters with swooping hands
and cracked off fingers   make her eat lots of
cream   make her eat lots and lots of ice-cream
Cora doesn't like ice-cream   back down to Nonnie
in Ecum Secum Eva sends her   Cora is so skinny
she cuts the whiskers off her cat

eyes but then she gets her legs

---

not the deaf one

Cora tells how Leonor wakes up screeching one
night so the man jumps out Eva's window and gets
his leg broken   it's the war you know   before Eva
gets poppy eyes and skinny legs   up and down the
back stairs up and down the back stairs Cora hears
Eva's visitors sneaking   she is hungry and itchy and
doesn't sleep so well   Orville is out on a destroyer
Eva gets so lonely   after the war she still gets lonely
for years and years   especially when Orville visits a
woman's house down on the Eastern Shore   after
the man jumps Leonor leaves Cora to live with
Nonnie and Nathaniel down in Ecum Secum
where there aren't any visitors   everyone goes to
bed at nine o'clock and if the telephone rings
Grampie Nathaniel jumps out of bed and hollers
who's dead

my great big mouth

at Eva's house Choral lives with her mother and Clarkie Cora goes away to work for a long time and someone takes Choral's hand walks her to the store buys her penny candy brown paper bag like snapshots she sees their wobbly bodies in the slumped store window Eva holds her hand Eva is Clarkie's mother Clarkie is four years older than Choral she keeps a snapshot of them hugging and laughing in front of the tinselled Christmas tree it's black and white with scalloped edges she thinks he's her brother laughs at them the neighbour laughs at them Clarkie is her uncle

I felt rate bad telling those two kids they weren't brother and sister, my god you should've seen their little faces crumple. It just flew rate out of my great big mouth. She's not your sister, Clarkie, I said laughing when he found me on the porch shaking the mop. Look Loretta, he hollered to me, I told you my sister would come back for a visit. She's not your sister, I said again. Well he's my brother, that little Choral spat at me, her left foot on the edge of a mud puddle getting her kneesock all over dirt. When she saw what she'd done she started screeching, my mother's going to strangle me, and I felt rate sorry for her. Come on in with me, I said, and I'll warsh it for you and nobody will know. To tell the truth, I wasn't sure if she meant her mother or her grandmother was going to strangle her 'cause she always called Eva Mumma, like the rest of them, and as far as I knew she called her mother Cora. But maybe that changed since Cora got herself properly married and moved away. I didn't want to ask after just opening my big mouth.

I gave them some molasses gems and warshed out her sock and laid it down hissing on the wood stove, watching Clarkie swing his legs back and forth. Reminded me of about four or five years back and he came over 'cause Cora was trying to wax the floor for Eva, she never did a thing herself far as I could ever tell. He was licking peanut butter off a spoon so I sat him rate up on the counter 'cause I was sweeping myself and he always was so cute swinging his legs like. I said, Clarkie whatchya got there, and he looks rate serious at his spoon and says plain as can be, shit, and went rate on licking away.

Now I know Cora must've told him peanut butter was shit, she had a mouth on her, boy did she have a mouth on her and you couldn't put it past her to be up to something. Like when she was going 'round with that young carpenter fella and give him a stick of Feen-a-mint one night hidden in a spearmint wrapper, and he was up and down his ladder all the next day 'cause they were putting a new roof on the old Crockett place.

That was while she was taking her business course before she worked over at the shipyard and got herself knocked up. Pardon me but plain truth's plain truth. She got herself knocked up.

There was some kind of screeching going on over there when Eva found out, let me tell you. Orville was out on the boat or he would've made her shut up.

What a bunch. There was no shame and no mercy.

All those kids were born at home except Clarkie. There was lots of gossip about him being one of the girls' babies but I think he was just a mistake, a change-of-life baby. Although even then, Eva never came out of the house too much and the girls were always going to stay with Eva's people down in Ecum Secum.

slice me up

for the last time before Cora takes Choral to live in the new house with Arthur her new husband Choral stays at Eva's sleeps in her bed Eva has a wine and gold puff all smooth and shiny soft with thick piping around the edges reversible in the night still dark Eva cries my hands are so swollen my hands are so swollen in the wine and gold light a man comes with a saw cuts off her rings in the wine and gold light Choral rubs her finger along the ruby ring Cora gave her last year but she can't feel the cut marks she can't get her rings off *get my rings off*

they tell Choral her father died in a car accident a month before she was born   searching for evidence of a dead father she roots around in closets and drawers   if there is a frosting rose from one wedding cake there will be a frosting rose from another   there's a stale hard rose from Cora and Arthur's cake (eat it anyway)   no old diamond rings or wedding pictures   no evidence of the dead father anywhere   he must be made-up   when she's four Choral decides Grace is her real mother but can't keep her because she works in a big bank in Toronto hold her mother to

- -

choke on my own vomit

Grace is in love with Jimmy McNeil   Eva won't let them get married because he's catholic   she says I don't mind coloureds but I can't stand catholics even before Grace marries Hank Norton she starts sticking her fingers down her throat after supper to throw it all up   and down her throat she still sticks her fingers even when she lives in Toronto and works in a big bank   she is really smart   her long black hair cut in a page-boy in Cora's wedding pictures   bony shoulders cords stick out on her neck Cora's hair bobbed bangs short under ruffled hat smiley face plump   a tooth missing the floor, push her mother to the floor

---

moves with and against

in the soft dim light Choral creeps into Cora's room
baby boy cooing in his crib next to the window oh
baby I'll feed you she whispers careful not to wake
her mother breathing through her open mouth
from dark room she slips to kitchen for a bottle
stacked in rows in fridge nipples turned upside
down little caps on top sshhh baby don't fret she
whispers standing on the side of crib reaching over
to touch his tiny lips with her tiny hands climbs
back down screws off cap turns nipple right side
up places bottle in ceramic bottle warmer on the
dresser sshhh baby do you need your diaper
changed she asks climbs back up bends over rail
pushing into her ribs and tummy as she pulls his
nightie up slides a pad under his bottom baby boy
whimpers when soggy rubber pants stick to his legs
she sticks pins in her mouth struggling sshhh
she spits through pins he watches her with dark
squinting eyes click she locks pins in place climbs
down to check bottle squirts a stream of milk on her
wrist still cool but warm enough under her arm
holds the bottle climbs back up on the rail slides
over the side into crib with the boy drags him into
a corner propping him between her legs sshhh
sshhh let mommy sleep she strokes his furry head

----

evidence, verisimilitude

Cora loses all her top teeth after her baby Ashton is born   nerve disease the old dentist says   happens all the time to pregnant women you can always tell if a woman's been pregnant by the state of her mouth   provides ether in his office pulls white shiny teeth   one by one white shiny teeth   she sleeps a lot stays in her room   wan   waiting for her new teeth   for one year she and Arthur have been married   when the teeth arrive special delivery from Halifax Arthur dances a little jig sings a little song   *Cor-ra's got her teeth a-gain teeth a-gain teeth a-gain Cora'sgotherteethagain lada da da dada* into the flesh, the curve, the arch

---

thrusts within and against

Cora wears a long pale pink ballgown no straps heart-shaped front back low tight up top and all puffy below with layers and layers of netting her hair black and short wears big round earrings and pink lipstick against a tall wooden stool she leans Arthur takes her picture with his Leica camera from England he develops and enlarges in black and white Cora always looks so pretty but sometimes they have awful fights at night about nasty naked pictures Clarkie found hidden in old tires in the cellar jesus jesus she screeches who the hell is that all shaved off

my ups and downs

while Cora is resting in her room Choral leans against the toilet practising a bow on her sneaker tying bows pulling laces little fingers winding and unwinding   pinching laces holding tight making loops squeezing loops together   trying to make the turn   pull the lace just right through the loop hold the loop   pull through   tired little fingers fidget thumbs lose grip she tries again   ahhhh she cries ahhhh   can't   leans her face against the toilet   toilet she says toilet toilet toilettoilettoi-let toilet over and over again until toilet slips to a sound until toilet means

the taste of blood in my mouth

in the cabinet over the sink is the gold mascara wand Choral climbs up to reach carefully twists it open sniffs the black magic goo makes your eye-lashes grow longer and thicker opens her eyes wide and round lifting her brows pulls down her cheeks and mouth lightly strokes her lashes alert for sounds in the hall listening downstairs hides away in the livingroom sits on the arm of the big red chair playing with a piece of string ties one end around her big toe the other around her pointy eye tooth tries to get her foot in her mouth balanc-ing tumbles down screeches and screeches blood spewing from her mouth Arthur and Cora rush to help searching for the lost tooth Arthur crawls on the floor first tooth to put under her pillow wish for Cora holds a cold cloth to her face wipes blood and tears and black streaks shakes her by the shoulders you little devil you've been into my mascara there won't be a dime from the tooth fairy for you you little devil and blood and blood spilling into

----

I can sing loud enough

the ocean shore along the ocean shore Choral drags a stick tracing her path in and out of waves in and out of wishes her sneakers wet steps along the rows of logs racked in shallows beside the wharf the tide is coming in the tide is coming in between the logs she spies a baby shark swimming piles stones and big rocks to pool him in crawls along the ledge of the wharf reaching for periwinkles stuck to the pilings fills her pockets to feed the shark his big teeth snap snap when she swishes her hand to pet him maybe he doesn't like periwinkles plump starfish pink and purple wash in the waves Choral gathers here sharkie she sings out loud plopping them into his pool nice juicy starfish for you the tide comes in over the rack over her feet she backs onto the beach builds a house by the boulders stone path rooms wild primrose windows watches her shark swim away as the waves rise over the rack the wishes

----

she dreams that up in the attic men with helmets and guns hold her mother to the floor, push her mother to the floor, flash a long knife, press the long blade into the flesh, the curve, the arch, the cusp of her achilles heel, slice broadly and deeply, blood and blood and blood spilling into

THE TESTIMONY OF ROXY FRENCH

It wasn't so much that her mother wouldn't let Grace marry Jimmy McNeil, it was that Grace married Hank Norton. She should have just come to Toronto by herself. I don't know what she needed a husband for anyway, she treated him like shit. But I bet she would've treated Jimmy McNeil like shit too after a while.

We were best friends in high school and when she called to ask about a job up here in the bank with me, I was delighted. It's not that easy to make friends in a big city and I thought it would be like old times. Her plan was to leave Hank and come up by herself. In the beginning we had a lot of fun. Grace was a real looker and heads would turn when she came into a room.

But then the phone calls started from Hank and before you knew it, up he comes and all our fun was blasted. Why'd she let him take her over again. She didn't even care that much for him. She never ever cared for anyone but herself, really. Wasn't capable. Down somewhere so deep she was stuck in all her little purses of pills and puking her guts up all day and still couldn't loosen that ruby she claimed to have swallowed.

Mumma's ruby is still growing inside me, she told me one night, sitting on the floor in a corner of my living room. One of those nights she arrived at midnight in a taxi, wrapped in her rose-coloured chenille housecoat, claiming Hank was going to kill her. More'n likely she was going to kill him. This happened every couple of months, usually on a Sunday. I'd try to get her calmed down and into the bed in the other bedroom and shut her up 'cause those cries of *Mumma look at me* would start the neighbours banging on the wall. I lived in a good building but if you could've heard her you'd understand. It wouldn't've mattered if I lived in a castle, you'd still hear *Mumma look at me.*

Jesus. And we had to go to work in the morning too. Those late nights never had much effect on her the first few years, she just got up the next morning as if we were having a pyjama party. I was the one dragging my ass. Grace was tough and smart. Not too many girls left the counter in those days but she worked her way up to assistant manager after about ten years. Mind you, ours was just a small suburban branch but you have to give her credit. Too bad she got herself so goddamned hooked on all those pills. And after her sister died she just got worse and worse.

By the time I moved into the duplex, I just couldn't have her arriving at all hours dressed in god-knows-what. That long hair of hers weedy and wild. She used to crawl her fingers along her scalp until it was slick with sebum, then work it out to the ends of her hair, pulling the grease through hairspray and stale smoke until you couldn't get too close to her without having a sick feeling in your gut. Christ. Then she'd coil huge hanks 'round and 'round on her fingers, till after a night of yanking on her hair she'd look like one of those gorgon pictures you see in movies. I just had to put a stop to her. She couldn't believe it when I wouldn't let her in anymore.

One of those nights back in the early years, I couldn't get her into bed. She just wouldn't budge from the floor where she sat cross-legged, clutching her big toes, rocking back and forth. Jesus murphy. But I finally figured out why she was wailing on about her mother's ruby all the time.

Seems when she was about three, the day Leonor was born, she stole her mother's ruby ring off a shelf in the bathroom. The wedding band and engagement ring were there too, apparently Eva had some kind of swelling in her hands. I don't know, I've never had a baby. But Grace took only the ruby ring, her mother's birthstone. There was such a commotion no one even missed Grace sitting under the back porch playing with the ring. Eva loved that ring 'cause Orville gave it to her and she was always, always crazy about Orville. When things quieted down and Grace could hear the new baby, she got scared. She thought God had brought the baby and that He might stay for a while to make sure everything was okay. She knew she had to put the ring back but couldn't for the life of her part with the beautiful red stone. So she picked and picked away at a loose claw until she dug the ruby out. Then for Christ's sake she ate it. She simply put the stoneless ring back on the bathroom shelf. No one ever figured out what happened. Orville had the stone replaced and that was that.

She could feel that stone grow and grow, Grace said. It grew long deep roots like the claws she stole it from, and swelled upward and outward till she was sure everyone who looked at her could see that red stone growing in her belly. And even when she didn't want the ruby anymore, she couldn't get rid of it. The ruby kept growing and growing, swelling and swelling.

Now this would want to make you laugh, she was so skinny. You couldn't imagine anything growing in Grace. Poor, poor woman, so good looking when she moved to Toronto but she just kind of eroded. Became bony, skeletal. Even her heart rhythms got so whacked out they put a pacemaker in.

In a magazine ad one time, I saw a picture of the inside of a seventeen-jewelled watch. I figured that's what Grace looked like inside too. A seventeen-jewelled watch, with little wheels and pins whirring around in her, all clicks and ticks that had to be wound up each morning. A smart gold watch with a slim oval face and hard ruby-clustered ovaries.

for an itchy monkey

so Cora can help out at Leonor's Arthur drops them
off for the day her baby is a couple of weeks old
Cora watches all the kids so Leonor can take a bath
in peace by the stubble of reddish hair sprouting
between Leonor's legs Choral is charmed the
apron flesh slung from her belly Leonor and Cora
swap birth stories compare marked bodies laugh
and laugh about a call-in radio show for home
remedies Leonor should call say I've just
had this lovely baby she's so sweet and everything's
okay I just have this one problem so I was wondering (she's supposed to say this really fast then get off
the phone) what do you do for an itchy monkey

on the couch in the strange room in the basement

---

depends upon and refuses

when Cora is just resting her eyes they play a game in a darkened room   on Cora's back Choral draws a cat a house an O   sometimes Choral has to nudge her   often Cora can't respond mumbles mmnn mmmnn   Choral traces the mark again squeezes soft flesh into lumps puckered like orange skin   the smell the mommy smell of her   be careful Cora moans   when Cora is just resting her eyes Choral combs and brushes her hair making ropes and knots   itchy all over she wants to get up   feels restless wants to play outside Cora murmurs scratch my back some more   by the end of the game Cora's back is criss-crossed with red welts   fat lines splash her soft soft skin so her mother gathers her into

---

my baby powdered bones

a party in the rec room in the basement in the winter children sleep upstairs in bedrooms in the livingroom on the couch in corners with bottles and blankets lights off noise loud from the party in the rec room in the basement arms tucked under toes crammed between cushions face down Choral lies on her belly in the dark a big fat man with his rum stink his pale scratchy face blunders into the room heaves his bulk onto the couch flattens Choral's face into rough cloth cushion can't breathe can't move man's muscle and flesh drown her skinny arms her skinny little legs her skinny little neck and ribs lungs squeak for air no breath no words can't get out the hot smelly bed and when her breathing creeps

---

between my legs and the wall

the first time Cora leaves Arthur   she and Choral stay in a hotel with the navy man from the party he gives Choral a rubber ball blue and red white stripe down the middle blue and red with a white stripe down the middle that she's not allowed to bounce   not allowed to bounce not allowed to talk too loud   no TV nobody to talk to   Choral chants softly *one two three o'larry four five six o'larry seven eight*   ring ring ring telephone rings from the lobby   not allowed to bounce a ball on the seventh floor of the Carleton hotel   Choral rolls the ball between her legs and the wall into the skin of her throat, body stilled

---

separate me and my heart

in the car Choral asks Arthur if she can live with him and the baby brother who is three and living with Lila for the meantime they're driving to visit with Lila for the weekend Choral roams familiar streets peeking in back gardens down a lane she rambles stands behind the house with the flower-pot garden where wild mint grows between paving stones she remembers it hot on her tongue and the hot welts on her bottom this was the place where she stayed too long one afternoon after the baby boy was born (didn't come home till after dark Cora didn't know where she was how could you do this to me how could you do this to me Cora cried when they found her you have to under-stand you can't wander around after dark we have to teach you a lesson you have to learn we're only doing this for your own good she raged as Arthur strapped her with his belt fat welts splashed her soft soft skin) lupines lupines everywhere clusters of purple pink mauve flowers on tall lively spikes Choral gathers in bunches the man cradles her mother's breast, strokes

---

the in between spaces around me

after lupines the navy man is gone forever Choral cannot remember the spacc between lupines and living back in the trailer in the woods along the shore Arthur and Cora and Choral and Ashton resume their Sunday afternoon drives eat chocolate bars Coffee Crisps Milky Ways Arthur and Cora smoke and smoke never stop the car never get out to walk along the rocks or shore except one afternoon Cora has to pee so bad they drive into a field along a bumpy road Cora squats by a bush another car drives into the field the driver man laughs and laughs to catch Cora squatted on the ground and Arthur laughs laughs laughs to find out how hot it is Choral sticks her finger into the cigarette lighter her mother's breast gently in time to

- -

letters sit on my bones

grade two Choral sits straight up second desk from front third row in the classroom in the basement looking out the high narrow windows onto the playground is a distraction an offence teacher says eyes front add ten plus six my name is read page read page Choral squeezes her knees presses her bum down looks straight ahead teacher opens her mouth and opens her mouth on a secret between her legs Choral sits squirms to look up out the window forget the navy man eyes front eyes front chokes the screech between her legs can't keep her eyes from the window teacher yells if you must look out that window Choral you can just put your desk up here up front so the class can watch you looking out the window move your desk up here between her legs straight up to her throat Choral chokes the screech his chest heaving, his belly breathing

---

of the two into one

during the Christmas holidays Arthur drops them off for the day   this is the next best place Eva lives   a big kitchen with sunny windows to view the bridge   Eva and Cora sit in the kitchen talk about god-knows-what drink tea   with a red pen Choral traces the swirly pattern on paper napkins   begs Eva to scratch her back with her long thin fingers and nice scratchy nails   when Clarkie comes home from the horror matinee they spread Leonor's old fur coats on the livingroom floor   plastic cabbage rose curtains closed   trace the blue veins on each other's legs with a blue pen   play hide and seek jump on the bed in Clarkie's room fall over each other bounce and jump   Choral is in love with Clarkie will marry him when she grows up her mother whispers, you know her father was

- -

reversible

too fast too fast Arthur drives his Morris Oxford too fast   Cora is afraid   Choral likes Arthur's cars (when she was little helped push the car up hills her hands pressing the dashboard push push he says there we go   wants to help him wash the car no no no can't help can't splash suds on his blue Austin buckets of water   little red boots   so mad so mad chops her hair off with Cora's kitchen scissors) one wet night Cora and Arthur get into a big fight driving around the rotary Cora screeches so mad so mad   she smashes him across the face breaks his glasses grabs his beard   hates him hates him can't stand this any longer   teach me how to drive

plug my listening pores

in the bathtub after Cora takes Ashton out Choral flips onto her stomach has the whole tub to herself stretches out rolls back and forth straightens out anchors the white floaty soap under her bum braces knees close to taps pushes feet hard against tub skids back and forth she is driving her car too fast suds and suds and suds foam from the motion the rocking Choral slicks herself with soap every smooth surface coated every crevice slippery itches itches reaches for the taps first the hot stings then the cold stings hot cold hot cold she pushes back and forth hot so hot stings like cold cold so cold stings like hot hot so hot turns to cold cold so cold turns to hot

---

she is afraid to sleep on the couch in the strange room in the basement so her mother gathers her into the hot smelly bed and when her breathing creeps into the skin of her throat, body stilled, the man cradles her mother's breast, strokes her mother's breast gently in time to his chest heaving, his belly breathing, her mother whispers, you know her father was never like this he was never like

It's probably true that if you love to dance you shouldn't marry a man who hates to dance. And Cora loved to dance. Lordy, she loved a good time and had a lot of fun in her. And sing, could she sing—*with a dixie melody*—as she always used to hum. That's how they met. She sang for a slapped-up little dance band, most of them couldn't even read music but they were enthusiastic. Arthur started picking up with them on weekends when the ship was in. He played that trumpet of his by ear. What a sight in those days. That black beard. Told us he grew it because of the scar on his jaw, but I'll tell you, he looked mighty out of place back then, 'way down here.

It was funny about him. We always served him tea 'cause he was an Englishman, but he didn't like tea at all and he never told us for years and years. And when Cora left the first time he was relieved to eat his tuna or salmon sandwiches with a bit of vinegar sprinkled on instead of mayonnaise. Now I ask you, wouldn't you think a person could let a person know about a simple thing like that.

Not that he wasn't mighty particular about other things, 'cause he was. Like his hi-fi set or his cars. The only things he brought with him from England were that three-piece hi-fi set he built and his jazz records. And his Leica camera. He got that Bolex movie camera of his up in Toronto when he first arrived, but couldn't afford to use it much after they got married. There's this one reel of film with all of us out at the beach when Ashton was just a baby, and I think some footage shows Choral helping him wash that little blue Austin of his. She loved to go in that car and he would pretend she was helping push it up the hill to the station. He always wore a sports cap and under the brim he would hide penny suckers. Called it his magic hat. Izzy whizzy let's get busy—suckers! he'd tease and then shake one out for her. She adored him and he was good to her, considering. But one time he got so mad when she scratched one of his records, he grabbed the small record player she played her red and yellow 45s on and smashed it down the basement stairs.

He was always taking pictures, developed them himself. He took some beautiful pictures of Cora and the kids too. It's too bad her little brother Clarkie found all those dirty pictures hidden in the basement. In old tires, for land's sake. Lordy lordy, who would have thought. What an episode. Now that I think about it, I guess he brought more than his hi-fi and records from England. He should have stuck to landscapes. My land, he took some lovely sunset pictures.

I think that's why they moved out of that first house. Bad memories. And the fact they were so far out of town. Cora was lonely in the daytime out there, couldn't even drive and afraid when he worked the night shift at the radar station. Sometimes she took Choral out there and they slept on mattresses on the floor, but when the station was painted with oil paint they had to stay home. Cora was pregnant and couldn't stand the fumes.

I think it was the loneliness that got her. All those years of waiting for him to come home. All those years stuck in the house with a couple of kids. Nowhere to go and nothing to do but cook and clean. She was a smart woman. Bored and lonely. That's a powerful bad combination. But at least back in those days she used to sing all the time. I can't remember the songs except for bits and pieces like *give me a pig foot and a bottle of beer* or something like *once I lived the life of a millionaire, spending money, I didn't care* while she worked around the house, cooking and bathing and dressing the kids. Sometimes we'd sit around and she'd play her little ukelele, let me see . . . *and you better not quarrel and you better not fight . . . let the midnight special shine its light on me.* Always singing. My land, she was always singing, *mmnnmm, nobody loves you when you're down and out.*

I don't know why they always seemed to live in the middle of nowhere when she couldn't even drive. Not that she'd have a car to drive anyway. But you'd think there'd be something she could figure out to do. Maybe it's like she said. Loneliness is a disease that can eat you alive.

Loneliness is worse than the monsters I used to see when I was a kid, she told me, 'cause when the loneliness gets me bad I don't see a damned thing. When the monster of loneliness grips me so bad, it's hard to fight back. I have to thrust my arms right out in front of me and stick my hands straight up so I can count my fingers to make sure I'm still here.

I'll never forget the time she came to visit after the Cuban missile crisis. The two of us were having a cup of tea in the kitchen and she nearly drove me crazy, tap-tap-tapping her little finger on the side of her cup. With her other arm hanging loose at her side, she'd tap those fingers with her thumb. Tap-two-three-four, tap-two-three-four. Like she was counting and counting I don't know what. Then she'd clench her fist and start all over again. Nearly drove me crazy.

She couldn't forgive Arthur for being away from home during that missile crisis. He travelled all the time. She'd make macaroni and cheese or beef stews 'cause Arthur hated that food. She begged him to stay home but he just laughed and said what difference would it make where he was if the whole East coast got blown to hell. It wouldn't matter. Well, it mattered to her. And to tell the truth, it would matter to me.

I'm just not sure why they moved and moved all the time. They were only here for three years and lived in four different places. Sometimes I think if they'd stayed put, things wouldn't have been so bad. Cora loved it here, she was the happiest I've ever known her. After they left she couldn't forget it. She always thought about moving back. What made her so happy was the distance she finally managed to put between herself and that family of hers. They were just far enough away that she couldn't be running over to them all the time, but not so far away she couldn't keep in touch. But Arthur was an ambitious man and he wouldn't just live out his life as manager at a radar station. He got a better job and had to travel. It's just too bad that put them right back within her mother's reach.

But why they had to keep moving house all the time I don't know.

Just like her mother. They had some kind of weird faith, like it was always going to be better in the next place or the next house, like all we have to do is find a good place and everything will be all right. Seemed like they couldn't stand to think about the present. Lordy me, I just never heard tell of people who moved so much, from place to place, house to house, and never seemed to get anywhere.

at night her feet get so hot she walks

I never get out of bed

at great-grandmother Nonnie's Choral dresses up in stinky old clothes   black stiff dresses flowered shawls with baldy fringes mouldy boots that hook up the front and umbrellas for parasols except they're rusty won't open   she pretends it's raining   there are way more clothes up in the back room   Uncle Stanley's   lots of stuff up there but no one's allowed to play or take stuff out   Uncle Stanley was the oldest of three a fine young man who drowned at twenty-one rolling logs in the harbour at the jamboree   Choral's heart thumps whacks hard in her skinny chest trying to get the creaky old door open so no one will hear her poke around in cracked trunks and stiff drawers that's how she knows about the clothes but she's too scared to take anything in case Uncle Stanley's guarding all that stuff   right under his old room is Nonnie and Grampie Nathaniel's bedroom   have to be really quiet they might be resting though when Choral thinks about it Nathaniel's quite deaf probably can't hear anyway gets so used to hollering at him she hollers at Nonnie too   Nonnie laughs and laughs at her I'm not the deaf one them up the wall or across the floor seeking

---

no longer coincide with myself

it's good to hear her laugh considering she's eighty just had her breasts cut off Choral and Cora and Ashton come to stay in Ecum Secum because Nonnie had her breasts cut off Nonnie won't let anyone except Cora change the dressings sometimes Choral is allowed in the bedroom when Cora bathes Nonnie changes the dressings like meat thawing on the counter with crusty edges and black stitches Nonnie's chest is all raw she turns her head away and pulls at the covers lives for five more years but never gets out of bed except to leave Ecum Secum that summer coolness, momentary coolness, gets up to pee

----

pinch my flesh back into place

Choral asks a doctor friend why they would cut off an old woman's breasts   for practice he says   now Nonnie and Nathaniel only come to Ecum Secum in the summer to the house built on a big flat rock the best smell is the wood bucket for bringing water from the well   old swollen wood   rusty metal straps taste of good dirt   the worst smell is the pantry in the sideboard Choral finds molasses cookies in a red and gold tin   must be a hundred years old hard as the whetting stone outside   puu-ee smells bad thick and sweet sweet   gets in her nose makes her body thick   the heaviest smell rises from chamber pots they keep under their beds for peeing only   pooping is for the two-holer out back   pee pots smooth and shiny decorated with pretty flowers lids that go clang   to pee in or just measure and admire   how much pee did you pee last night strong yellow pee that smells like piss rests hot feet on cool floor, moves them

---

for practice

in the front room   a horsehair couch fern table and the pump organ Nathaniel gave Eva   Choral pecks *do re mi* pulls out every other knob presses her hands flat on the keys pumps her feet hard   wants to play a tune pump her feet   doesn't know how hums the only organ song she knows   *dum dum da dum   dum da dum   da dum   dadum*   plays it over and over again   *dum dum da dum   dum da dum   da dum   dadum*   what do you think you're doing Cora scolds   Nonnie's not deaf you know she's just in the next room   that's a dirge you're playing Choral doesn't know what a dirge is except it's something you're not supposed to play on the pump organ when someone gets their breasts cut off around as floor heats up, in bed feet burn

---

neither sex nor death

under the covers in the house down the road from Nonnie and Nathaniel's Choral's cousin tells how her big sister and the boy from the gas station play games in the back room at night with water and perfume the cousin pulls the covers up over their ears the smell of old piss hot and thick she grips Choral's nightgown at the hip whispers he spreads her legs wide open when she sits on the edge of a chair he pours hot hot water from the kettle down there with her finger so close to the spot that warms between Choral's legs the cousin points hush but first he dabs perfume from a dark blue bottle on her hair down there so it won't stink so bad when the hot hot water pours down between her legs to the floor

squeeze myself out

down the dark hall   between Nonnie's room and the front room   near the pantry Choral squats on a chamber pot practising her ups and downs   an old lady down the road gave her white bone knitting needles and some odd balls of wool   showed her how to put the stitches on   make her rows of ups and downs   hard to knit in the dark hall she keeps losing stitches   starts all over again counting the stitches counting the rows   holes and knots doesn't hear Nathaniel sneak down the hall   what's this what's this he cackles pointing his finger at her squatting   rumbles off to tell everyone   cackles and cackles

I learn to breathe

off to the swimming hole sneak Choral and a cousin
Choral can't swim takes a rubber duck float ring
paddles into deep water far over her head blackflies buzz and nip her neck cousin searches the
shoreline for yellow water lilies Choral swats
blackflies crawling in her ears and slips through
duck into dark lake down she sinks down cold
water surprises her wide open eyes around and
around she turns in this soundless heavy world
sputters flaps arms and legs struggling for shore
head pokes through a tangle of water lily reeds pulls
herself out of water crying trudges through
woods to Nonnie's house tells Cora she knows
how to swim now

at night her feet get so hot she walks them up the wall or across the floor seeking coolness, momentary coolness, gets up to pee, rests hot feet on cool floor, moves them around as floor heats up, in bed feet burn, she imagines buckets of cool water dark and musky

We were on the move so much when I was a kid, it's hard to keep track. When we were little we lived in Shipton. That's where Aunt Sophie went after she left Ecum Secum and met up with Kippy, Dad's brother. Kippy stayed around just long enough to get Aunt Sophie pregnant. I guess there was some hullabaloo over that one. You can imagine. Nonnie never even so much as put lipstick on in her life and Grampie Nathaniel was such a straight hard man, it's a wonder they didn't disown her. But Aunt Sophie was always the favourite and at least she was far enough away that everyone down there didn't have their noses rubbed in it.

It's hard to believe they let Mumma go to stay with her when the baby was born. And it sure didn't take long for her and Dad to get married. I guess she didn't want a mess like poor old Sophie. Always claimed she was a virgin when she got married and she never let any of us forget it.

When we were little Dad joined the navy and moved us to Dartmouth. We lived there till Mumma got pregnant with Clarkie and then moved back to Shipton. Mumma was scared. In her forties, you know. When I complained about moving again, she told me, Cora I need to be near your Aunt Sophie in case anything goes wrong.

What miserable old things they were. The two of them, all hunched over in the kitchen, saying god-knows-what about everyone. Mumma would whine 'cause Dad was never home and Aunt Sophie would say, well at least he's been home in the last few years, at least you've still got the support of a husband, and then Aunt Sophie would whine about her job at the laundromat and Mumma would say, well, at least you can look after yourself. And if they weren't talking about someone they were complaining about their health. There was always something wrong with one of them or both of them. Christ, one year the whole bunch were all in the hospital at the same time. Gall-bladders or hysterectomies or something. Seemed like their whole lives were recorded in doctors' files or stitched into the scars on their bodies. How the hell could anyone ever keep track.

Not that Nonnie was a complainer. God love her. You could always depend on Nonnie unless she was having one of her fits. She was a lovely quiet woman, a woman of true repose. Except if she got mad at Grampie Nathaniel. He had better treat her good or she would just fly into him and then he'd run out and get an armload of wood or a bucket of water. She was the only one who ever opened a mouth to him. He was a miserable old bastard. Always on his high horse. The only ones he ever cared about were Aunt Sophie and Leonor. The rest of us could just go to hell.

Never allowed to talk at the table. Even all those years later, when we visited after Nonnie's operation. My poor little Ashton had to sit on the left side of that miserable old son-of-a-bitch and he taunted him, hollered at him. Imagine. Ashton was only four years old. I finally lit into him. Listen Mister, I said, no one treats my little boy like that.

The year before we moved back to Shipton I lived down in Ecum Secum again. That was an awfully good year. Nonnie always made foxberry pies for me and I learned to separate milk from cream. That was about as much as Grampie Nathaniel would let me do. He was an old reprobate but he would never let a woman pick up even so much as a big platter of food. I always figured that's what made Mumma and Sophie so damned useless.

I came back home when Grace started to get so thin. She used to be a big girl, like Dad's side of the family. Every night she went into the bathroom to throw up everything she'd had to eat that day. When she finished high school she got a job at the bank and married Hank. On the rebound 'cause Mumma wouldn't let her go around with Jimmy McNeil. He was catholic.

Hank was a drunk. And then Grace started to drink. I was glad when they moved to Halifax but then they'd come home to Shipton for the weekends. God knows why, all they did was drink and fight. Mumma would get into it. Never could hold her liquor. Grace would be bawling and crying and then Mumma would be bawling and crying. What a mess. We couldn't even have Christmas without all that mess.

It never stopped.

One weekend Jimmy McNeil came nosing around and of course he and Hank got into a great big fight and I ended up squished behind a door and Mumma had to call over to Aunt Sophie to come quick 'cause she didn't know what to do. She was always calling on her to tell her what to do. What a pair. As if Aunt Sophie had managed her life so well. But it made old Sophie strut like the cock-of-the-walk in a house full of blubbering hens. She wasn't even five feet tall.

My goodness gracious I didn't have fits. I had epilepsy. I didn't fly into Nathaniel either, but I could make him back up. Yessirree. A trick I learned from an old cat. She was about twelve when we got this great big dog and he would lunge for her. But she would march right toward him with her ears flat and if he didn't back up, she'd swipe at his snout with her claws. It's a pity my poor Eva never learned to do that. Those beautiful long fingernails of hers. She should have let that fool husband of hers have it across the snout.

Maybe Cora is remembering the time I was stricken by the snake out on the back porch. I had gone with the teapot, ready to throw out the dregs, then a snake stole across my foot and I couldn't move. Paralysed. That's how they found me. Like a stone angel holding a teapot. Really, I have to confess those fits weren't so bad. At least I got to get away for a while.

There were other teapots too. The teapots that flew around the house in Tangier before I married Nathaniel. Not only teapots but bowls and forks and knives. We used to think it was the ghost of my twin who died. Two months premature and so small they put me in a red and gold Christmas tin and set me behind the stove to keep me warm and alive. My twin. A girl. Born dead. Funny expression, isn't it. Born dead.

That red and gold tin sat on a shelf in the pantry all our married life. Full of molasses cookies. Nathaniel shouldn't have sold the old place without letting all the girls take what they wanted first. Cora should have had that tin. She was so gentle and so attentive after my operation. By the way she put her hands on me I knew she was just as bewildered as I was about the hack job they did. I never ever imagined that so much of my flesh would be removed. I could tell the others thought it didn't matter about an old woman like me. But Cora had the right touch.

I wish my twin had said say hello in our house on the flat rock. If it was possible for the dead to visit I'm sure Stanley would have come to say good-bye. My firstborn, you know, my little boy. Drowned. How could that be, I could never quite believe it. I locked up all his things in his room praying he would come back and move them around so I would know he was there. All the grandchildren and great-grandchildren swore the upstairs was haunted because of Stanley. But it wasn't. Stanley never moved a thing. Those children loved to sneak in there, snoop around, open drawers and trunks. I always knew they were up there, not Stanley. My poor, poor Stanley. We never got to say good-bye. Mercy me.

The upstairs wasn't haunted. What they felt was my sorrow and Leonor's rage. Her poor baby with holes in his heart. Imagine. There she was, out picking blueberries and comes home to find her baby dead. Only sixteen. No no. Sadness and rage lived upstairs. Not Stanley. Not even little David.

The summer I had my breasts cut off was the last summer I laid in my own bed, listening to the children upstairs, opening and closing old drawers and trunks. I should have told them to take what they wanted. They never got another chance. Why did it make Nathaniel so mad about anyone being up there. I should have just told the old fool to let them be. What could I possibly have been afraid of then. I lived but I never walked again. Those fool doctors. I should have been more like that old cat and made them back up instead of letting them practise on me. So I ended up with five years to practise. Practised flying teapots around in my head and practised flying away, like when I had fits. But I never practised being deaf like Nathaniel.

there she sits in the kitchen, hasn't seen

---

the pleasure of you

the only time Choral ever sees Eva outdoors is sitting on the steps of the yellow house on Gaston Road   this is the best place she lives   Eva likes to sit in her kitchen drinking cup after cup of bitter black tea   she runs outside because Clarkie lost his snake   she and Cora are in the kitchen when Clarkie bounds in   did anyone see my snake   they jump and screech   there are a lot of snakes around here   Clarkie and Choral like to hunt them down in an old black lunch can with grass he keeps his snake   for comfort   Eva's soft brown dress with rabbit fur pom-poms to play with when she holds Choral on her lap

Leonor for twenty-five years, can almost

---

stop and look at myself

Orville is back in town   the best joke is when he gets off the boat gets into a taxi asks   where do I live now   Leonor and Archie are back from Germany   to look at all Eva's bottles and jars   Choral locks herself in the bathroom   there's nothing to do might as well wash the walls   underneath the stripes she makes on the grimy walls with a face cloth and pink camay is bright yellow   in the kitchen Orville sets her on his lap to watch his girlfriend dance   a blue and red mermaid who wiggles with his arm muscles his rum stink his grey scratchy face   in the bedroom trying on new clothes Cora and Leonor turn to shut the door   Orville hollers don't think I haven't seen your bare asses before touch her round face, dyed red hair, smell her

----

as a presence that precedes

in the apartment over the bake shop on Portland Street   that's where Leonor sees Eva walk to the bathroom in the middle of the night   Vivian comes back to work for thirteen dollars a week   she sees Eva too   Eva needs a hired girl because she won't walk anymore   Choral knows Vivian is nineteen because Cora says   how can anyone nineteen have so many problems she has to get tranquilizers   she doesn't know what problems are   Cora is thirty Choral is ten   Vivian has a typewriter in her small room off the kitchen   lets Choral type (she thinks Vivian's okay)   years later Clarkie tells her about his first screw in that room with Vivian (he was fourteen)   she keeps saying don't come don't come he says I won't I won't last cigarette, taste her beery kiss, Leonor tells

---

my sprawling stretched out words

Eva has pale scratchy furniture in the latest style a sectional arranged in lots of ways but always nubbly on the legs on the floor sit black and white poodles Junior won at the fair Choral wishes he'd win some for her Eva likes to watch wrestling and *Hymn Sing* on TV or talk to Mrs. Joseph on the phone her best friend Choral never meets no one ever meets Mrs. Joseph on Eva's bed with the wine and gold puff Choral lies reading her *True Confessions* while they wait for the boy to come for their order pop and chips and candy bars plus cigarettes for Eva the boy gets twenty-five cents Choral wants Eva to give her the beautiful pink fan she keeps in the middle drawer of her vanity bureau be careful be careful Eva always says be careful with my beautiful pink fan Choral and Ashton stay with Eva when Cora goes to the hospital to birth Fern Choral dresses up in all Eva's scarves and big round earrings she finally gives Choral the beautiful pink fan and soon after Choral loses it somewhere

Cora I saw Mumma walk to the bathroom

---

silent in the nether world

the best thing about Eva is her long fingernails on her long tapered fingers   ruby ring and diamond ring thin gold wedding band   aristocratic someone says   guess that comes from her mother's mother Caroline Conrad daughter of a Marquis (or something) from Scotland   who ran away with the gardener   a French Huguenot named Gaston (they eloped to Tangier along the Eastern Shore)   that's why she doesn't like to do any housework   when Eva scratches Choral's back   long fingernails on long tapered fingers   Choral imagines her great-great-grandmother with beautiful soft hands sailing on a ship from Scotland with her secret lover in the middle of the night, but that's not what

---

I've come to tell you

Eva walks into the apartment over the bake shop but she doesn't walk out   that's why Vivian then Mrs. Turple come   Mrs. Turple can't stand it   Eva gets Vivian back because the poor poor thing needs a place to go   since she got out of the mental hospital   she mostly keeps Eva company can't keep that place clean can't get that place clean   not with Clarkie's rabbit pooping all over and the grasshoppers he guillotines   Choral doesn't know what they eat   doesn't seem to be any food   the weekend she stays when Nonnie dies   makes a chocolate cake mix with gobs of frosting that's what they have for supper   Eva doesn't go to Nonnie's funeral because her legs are so bad and Choral's not allowed to go because she's twelve

----

something tangled about my mother

before Nonnie finally dies they're sure she's going to die one other night   Arthur drives Cora and the kids to Eva's apartment   peeling paint around all the windows   street light shines dingy rainbows on the gas-slicked street   Cora makes them wait outside   sure as hell doesn't look forward to breaking the news to Eva (they always make her do these things she'll be so glad when they move far away again so she can finally get the hell away from them all)   Nonnie will die that night   Eva carries on moaning and wailing   she carries on and on   I never want to do that again Cora grumbles when she gets back in the car

---

there she sits in the kitchen, hasn't seen Leonor for
twenty-five years, can almost touch her round face,
dyed red hair, smell her last cigarette, taste her beery
kiss, Leonor tells Cora I saw Mumma walk to the
bathroom in the middle of the night, but that's not
what she comes back to tell me

Oh oh oh poor Eva. Those girls always gave her such a hard time. Never listened to her, never paid her any attention at all. Now the boys were a different matter altogether. Junior and Clarkie were always good to their mother. Every time she bailed Junior out of trouble, lent him money or took him in off the streets, every time, he told her how much he loved her and did little things for her. Like going to the store. And little Clarkie, why he cooked for her 'most every night and even brought her the bedpan. Especially after her legs started getting bad.

That was a terrible thing, her legs going like that. Terrible thing for a woman in her prime. Those girls could've done more for her. I'll admit Cora stopped by whenever she could get her husband to drive her. But Grace, Grace could've come home from Toronto more often. Eva didn't see her for years. And that Leonor. What a little witch she was. Settled herself in with Eva when it suited her, even had the two little girls with her one time. I don't know where the boy was or that no-good husband of hers. She wouldn't do a thing for her poor mother, not even bring her the pan. Told her to get up and walk to the bathroom like everyone else. Those were terrible times.

Eva called me every day and it was just enough to make you cry. She couldn't get out 'cause of her legs and I was doing poorly myself. So we called each other every day, sometimes a couple of times a day. Between our programs.

Our husbands were in the navy together. Orville was as strong as an ox and I don't think anything could have felled him. My husband wasn't so lucky and they were rate good to me after he was killed. We had real problems in those days. Not like now.

If it hadn't been for the war I'm sure poor little Junior would have made more out of himself. Had his father's charm and good looks. They were all good looking. Except Leonor. Anyway, Junior was brought up by a bunch of women and I guess they spoiled him. But they were mean to him sometimes too. Just before his fifth birthday he was leaning out an upstairs window cussing them as they left for school. And didn't the window slam down on his head and just about cut his tongue off. Hanging from a thread. And the blood. Poor Eva had to take a taxi to the medical centre and they managed to sew it back on. Whath's up little Orfille, Orfille Ju-ni-or, Orfille baby, canth you eat your birfhday cake. Cath's got your tongue, those girls teased him for a whole week.

He never gave his mother any trouble. Well, maybe just that once. After Eva and Orville moved back to Shipton for a while. Junior called me up to say that Eva was dead. Oh oh oh I was beside myself. I called poor Sophie up to tell her how bad I felt and she didn't know what on earth I was talking about. I felt rate stupid. I think even Eva was a little put out. Why in the world Junior would do such a stupid thing we could never figure out.

She had a hard life. Those girls always snickering behind her back, raising their eyebrows like *she's not too bright, you know*. I don't think that was the problem. More like she dropped a stitch somewhere along the way. Just let her whole life get knit up around her, couldn't even see where she was ravelling out. And nobody knew to pick up the hook and loop her back in.

She had this funny little laugh, *ahehehe*, when she couldn't figure out what was going on. Someone would say something and she would just sort of twitter *ahehehe.* Like a bird. Maybe it was all those pills she took for the thyroid. She had such big blue eyes but the thyroid took its toll on them. Over the years they grew bigger and bigger and looked hard as rocks. It could have been the thyroid caused her legs to go bad, but then maybe it was because she didn't eat too good. She never had much of an appetite.

Mostly smoked and smoked. Just sat and smoked in her rocking chair, waiting for something to happen or Orville to come home. Oh oh oh she worshipped him. Sometimes he didn't come home for years at a time. He even lived with another family way down the Eastern Shore, but she always waited for him. The patience of an angel is what she had. Sometimes I thought she'd turn to stone waiting for him.

But whatever it was that was wrong with poor Eva, those girls could have done more for her. I'll never know why on earth they treated their own mother so poorly.

when she brushes

---

the noise of my pain

in the kitchen Leonor and her friend sit with Cora
laugh drink beer and Arthur's scotch   make us
beautiful they say   with Arthur's razor Choral cuts
their hair sets it in rollers teases it   high   on
the table they spread out compacts bottles make-up
tubes and pencils   smoke stings Choral's eyes   she
brushes eye-shadow on Leonor and even though she
pulls the eye-lids tight her skin is all crinkly   the
soft brush rolls her skin around like chicken skin
Leonor is thirty-three   Choral is fifteen   figures if
she looks very close in the mirror every day   if she
keeps watching   her skin can't get like that

Leonor's hair the whole scalp

---

my noisy skin

Ashton's birthday party   outside little boys playing loud games   Choral upstairs getting ready to go out   Cora answers the phone the sounds she makes Choral can't even call screeching   the *noo-ooonnooooo* she makes comes from all over her body not just out her mouth   the *nooooonnooooo* is as wide and deep as her flesh   Choral hears *nooooonnooooo* runs downstairs can see the sound and taste and breathe nothing else   *noooooooooo-ooo* trips every cell in their bodies   clamps down on the news that Leonor is dead lifts behind the ear because they

---

couldn't stand to look out

Leonor gets a job as a cocktail waitress she is soft and round and laughs looks smart in the black and white uniform with her dyed red hair makes good tips that she keeps in one of Nonnie's old jars in the kitchen saving up for the kids should be a good Christmas this year for a change loves that little Pekingese dog too that's why Cora can't believe she committed suicide can't believe no one was looking out for her Leonor gets so sick to her stomach and doesn't sleep so she takes tranquilizers and is sleeping so hard when she throws up she chokes to death on her own vomit *tucked away all by myself*

up to Leonor's Cora takes her best dress the silky one cool green and sandy with the fern pattern that looks good with Leonor's red hair Cora fixes her make-up and hair too beause they always over-do it in those places she says from top to bottom they slit the dress drape around her tuck in at the sides (to perform an autopsy the body is slit from top of skull to base of spine they just dig every-thing out then stuff the body with something) so the dress fits right of course there is no reason to use the matching belt so Cora and Choral take it home

what I was after

Cora allows Choral to go on the train with her and Grace to Eva's after the funeral   Arthur doesn't think Choral should go because she's missed so much school   she's never been on a train before wants to attend Eva again   her face   poppy eyes ask if she remembers the beautiful pink fan   watch if she cries   listen to the funeral talk   all the details how they found Leonor drowned in her own vomit how could it happen   how is Archie going to cope with four kids the baby only eleven months old (they're not even all his kids)   Eva didn't go to the funeral because her legs are really bad now and Choral had to look after all of Leonor's little kids when she brushes Leonor's hair the whole scalp lifts behind the ear because they forgot to sew it back together

All I wanted to do was look at the beautiful fan Dad brought home for Mumma. It wasn't very big. Fragile. Perhaps ivory. Such a delicate shade, pale pink. I would sneak in her bedroom whenever I could. Like going into a cave 'cause she always kept the curtains closed. Her bureau had three drawers down each side, with a small sunken drawer that made a bridge between them. That's where she kept the beautiful pink fan. And nothing else. A large oval mirror was attached to the bridge and under the bridge fit a padded bench. I was still small enough to hide in that space the day she found me.

The fan had a fancy pattern of lacy holes that split the space of the room into a million pieces if you held it close to your face and squinted. Mumma always had that wine and gold shiny puff on her bed, and wine and green cabbage rose curtains. The light in there was heavy and close. I was sitting on the bench facing the mirror with the fan spread open, practically resting on my nose, breathing in her dark blue perfume. Just letting my eyes roll across the lacy pattern, slowly opening and slowly closing so all the little holes danced around the room. I crossed my eyes to let everything go into soft focus. Let my lids drop to stare through one hole and looked into the mirror and jesus, *there was Mumma*. She was behind me and in front of me at the same time. Leonor, she screeched. I thought her great big poppy eyes were going to explode and splatter into my face and onto the mirror.

I didn't have a bureau in my room down in Ecum Secum. Just an orange crate standing on its end, with a cotton print skirt and painted top. Beside the old iron bed. I hung my clothes on wall hooks. After

Archie and I got married, we put up more hooks. Nonnie and Grampie Nathaniel wouldn't let me go 'round with the young boys I liked, said I was safer with Archie 'cause he was so much older. Now wouldn't that make you want to laugh.

When David was born we fixed up a square galvanized washtub with padding and I made a cute little skirt for it to match the orange crate. You really couldn't tell the baby's bed was a washtub. We were saving up for a crib, there just wasn't enough time.

They said it was my little boy who died 'cause he had holes in his heart. But it was me, too. I had holes in my heart. I died a long time ago. They thought they could see right through me, but they never saw the holes.

The thing you have to know about Leonor is she was restless. Always on the move. Always thought things were going to get better. Most of the time, anyway. There was that awful time she told me about, happened years ago. She was living down on the Eastern Shore somewhere around Tangier, Moose River maybe, and she took all those sleeping pills. I just wanted to sleep for a long time, she told me. Arthur drove Cora all the way down there, waited outside with the kids for hours while Cora held her hand and helped pull her through.

Cora came to the rescue more than once and it made for a lopsided relationship. Cora the strong one, Cora the beautiful one, Cora the one with the fancy husband. Oh Leonor needed her alright, but she sometimes felt like she lost more than she needed in the first place. Especially if money was involved. Like the time she talked Cora into asking Arthur to co-sign a loan for Archie and of course he screwed up and Arthur ended up paying the whole thing. At a finance company no less; interest rates were damned high. Leonor and Archie got bailed out but a barrier was built that never got completely torn down. Cora resented Leonor putting her in such a predicament and Leonor resented that Cora was married to someone who could pay his bills and someone else's too. And who the hell knows what Arthur resented. It's hard to imagine he didn't make life hell for Cora over that one. They were pretty strapped for cash themselves. Of course a thing like this would only deepen his bewilderment about the kind of family he had married into. But he had his little secrets too, didn't he.

When Leonor had Sandra, she didn't have so much as a receiving blanket. Out Cora went and bought enough clothes for her to bring the baby home from the hospital. I can't remember where Archie was that time.

I didn't know Leonor then, only met her when they moved to the base. We both had little dogs we walked in the morning after the kids went to school, otherwise I wouldn't have met her. She stayed in the house all the time and always, always kept the curtains closed. When I asked her once why she never opened them to let in some light and fresh air, she just laughed and started talking about something else.

My husband was in Germany and Leonor was lonely so we spent a lot of time together. You know how it is when you meet someone and you can talk and talk and talk. Like falling in love. You want to know everything about that person and you feel like you can tell them anything.

I was on a diet and lost a lot of weight, to surprise my husband when he got back. Leonor gave me a whole closetful of clothes from when she was thinner. See, first she was pregnant with her last baby and then she went and got that job as a cocktail waitress. She never fit back into her old clothes. I even think some of the clothes were from Cora. Those two. Always changing weight, up and down, up and down. And they'd always give their clothes to someone who they thought might need them or want them. Each had a drawer full of different-size bras on hand, depending on how fat they were. They usually kept the bras.

Cora used to call Leonor long distance all the time and Arthur would give her shit for talking so long, but she just kept right on making the calls. Leonor called too, but not as often. She couldn't get away with it. Though now that I say that, it sounds funny 'cause Leonor could get away with just about anything.

That mother of hers accused her of some pretty mean things, but it's not true that all her kids had different fathers. Though perhaps it could have been. Leonor loved men and men loved Leonor. Oh she was really something alright, even when she was putting on weight. I think it was her smile, her mouth. When Leonor smiled at you she smiled with you, she took you in and made you warm. Her smile said, you'll be okay with me. And she moved her body toward you like a gift you'd waited for all your life. I think Cora was like that too, but she had an edge to her. Maybe she was too smart. I don't know.

Not that all her loving ever made Leonor happy. Not by a long shot and not for long anyway. She had her moments. There was this fellow down in Moose River who was crazy about her, they were all crazy about her, and she talked him into taking this cat she found. One day he came into her place pissed off saying, that cat Mitchy you gave me is no Mitchy and now I've got six kittens to get rid of. She just laughed at him and kissed him sweet and he left thinking six kittens were a joy to behold. No one would think of drowning kittens if they were connected with Leonor.

She always found men who would do anything for her, but she always came back to Archie. I hate to think how hard it must have been on those poor kids. Dragged around from post to pillar. Poor little buggers. She always wanted to do her best for them. She just didn't seem to know what the best was. Couldn't make a judgment in a world, her world, that held no justice, no rhyme or reason. We used to get pissed together sometimes and she'd say, it's so damned hard to figure out what to do, I can't seem to open a door that won't slam in my face. I can't open a door that I can close myself. I don't know why everything has to be so damned hard all the time. And then she'd feel sorry for herself and she'd feel sorry for me and sorry for you. And she'd cry for all of us.

One thing that really made her sad was the fact that the last baby wasn't Archie's. His real father was a nice man from Sanction Harbour who loved Leonor and offered her the world to come live with him. He wasn't even married, never had been. Not like that mess Cora got herself mixed up in. Leonor told me all about how Choral's real father was a right two-timer. Already had a wife and four kids. Imagine. Anyway, when Leonor wouldn't go with the man from Sanction Harbour, he wanted to make sure the baby would always be provided for, wanted to have Leonor sign documents swearing he was the father so he could leave everything to him, provide for him. But she wouldn't, said that would make her son illegitimate and she couldn't do that to him.

It all turned out okay 'cause Archie always loved those kids, each and every one of them. Held them together. Maybe that's what Leonor thought, that the kids belonged together. I remember she said that no matter what happened in the world, she always had Cora. Even Grace and Junior and Clarkie were counted as what she had in the world that belonged to her, after her grandparents died.

One Sunday morning Leonor and I drove down to Cora's. Those two were so happy when Cora and Arthur moved close, an hour-and-a-half drive was nothing. Still, it was hard to find the time to get together. We had a ball. Cora got out Arthur's scotch and a few beer to chase it down. We sat at the kitchen table smoking and laughing. Choral joined us for a while. Cut my hair and set it, did a fine job for a teenager. Then made us all up in that eye-shadow and eye-liner she wore all the time. We had to talk her into putting lipstick on us too

’cause that wasn’t the rage for her group. They were all eyes. Oh that red mouth of yours, she said to Leonor when she’d got her all dolled up. I could hardly wait to get back and show that husband of mine how glamorous his special Sall could look.

Archie told me to take all Leonor’s things, all her clothes. I had to ask if Cora wanted anything, but I already knew the answer. Cora didn’t want Leonor’s things, she wanted Leonor. At the funeral the minister told me that when he called Cora to break the news, he had never in his career, never in his life, heard such a sound as the sound she let off. A sound that rode through her body, clawed her throat, scraped out the top of her scull. Like an unnameable animal, he said.

I don’t know how she managed. How in the name of god she found the strength to tend to the dead body of her own dear sister. I guess it took a hell of a lot of love and courage to brush Leonor’s hair, fix her make-up, dress her in that soft green dress she brought.

I kept the curtains closed because I couldn't stand to look out. I couldn't stand to look out and I couldn't stand the idea of anyone looking in. What was there to look out at anyway. By the time we moved to the base I was bone tired. Bone tired. And that was before my last poor baby was born. By the time I brought Clary home from the hospital my face was numb with weariness. Archie helped out with meals and dishes and the other three kids were pretty good, but god love them they still needed attention. I probably shouldn't have taken that job as a cocktail waitress, I was too tired to do my lot at home let alone at some crummy bar, but I had to get out. I had to get away. And there's no use pretending we didn't need the money. We needed the money. There was just never enough. Especially after the kids got into their teens, they needed more and more and more of everything. And anyway, I liked the shiny black dresses we wore, even if I was spilling out all over. Beat the hell out of slacks and a striped blouse day in and day out. The company might have been a little rough down there sometimes, but it was a change. A change is as good as a rest, they say.

Wouldn't the world be a damned fine place if that was the truth.

I could have used a rest. A real rest. Cora was always saying she was going to take off and go live in the woods where nobody would find her. I sure as hell knew what she meant. You can get just about anything you think will help: booze, pills, food, sex, anything at all you think will help. But you can't get a rest. You can't get it for love nor money. It's nowhere to be found.

I liked coming home when everybody was asleep. I liked just to sit in the front room in the dark and have a couple of beer in the silence and peace. I didn't even have to think 'cause my muscles and bones and skin beat out a weary tune, a throb throb throbbing. I only had to think, these are my muscles, this is my skin, these are my bones. The song of my clamouring body was all the company I could stand. I would hold my head in my hands and rub rub rub the flesh of my face up and down on my hard hard skull and it was hard to think they belonged together. When the momentary peace started to edge away I felt my skin, muscles and bones start to edge away too and I'd make my hands knead and pinch my flesh back into place. Then I'd lose all track of time and doze in and out of sleep holding myself together on the couch. Sometimes I'd stay there all night and sometimes I'd find the strength to hoist myself up into bed and I always, always prayed the baby would sleep for a couple more hours.

So I went on like that for god knows how long and then people would talk to me but I couldn't put all the words together, my mind would bounce them all back out and the words would scatter all around my feet. I couldn't even send them back to where they belonged. All my own words slid out of my mouth and sprawled wherever they could but they were so stretched out I don't think anyone could shape them. I practised gathering the words back in and patting them into shape but I couldn't get a nice round shape that someone could catch. It seemed I could only make blocks out of the words, like baby blocks, and I couldn't spell anything, I could only make letters. So I stacked them like the towers you make for babies and the first block I placed deep inside my womb and I reached out for my sprawling stretched-out words and I tried and tried to round them and I tried and tried until my insides felt weak and bursting, so I gave in and made the blocks blocky and stacked them to pad and prop all my bursting insides. None of the letters made sense, I still couldn't make a word, so I had this tower of letters that made no sense building up inside and they started pushing against my lungs and I'd forget to breathe I was so charmed with the blocky push on my chest. Then my heart would beat hard to get my attention so I'd take a deep breath and the space just started filling up all on its own with all these blocks, I couldn't stop them and they blocked my heart and separated it from the rest of me and my heart would beat out to push them away but the blocks pushed back harder and for weeks I went around with this fight in my chest and I couldn't make the letters right to spell out two little words. I was trying to build two little words for someone to hear but the blocks had taken over and they were filling me and there was no more room and my chest was being punched out from the inside and the blocks just stacked right up into my throat and I couldn't get a breath down I was just breathing at the top of my throat, heart and lungs were screeching for air so I drove my thumbs into my chest and squeezed and dug my thumbs into my ribs from the outside, I pried at my ribs from the outside to let in some air but the blocks with the letters sat on my bones, I couldn't pry them loose, I couldn't get the air in the space in my throat it filled up with blocks and blocks the edges were hurting I tried to press the edges back in with my fingertips but my fingertips cracked off so I pressed the stubs of my fingers into my throat but they didn't have the power to push back the edges I couldn't breathe, I was so tired and then I knew all I had to do was get some rest and throw up all the blocks.

All I had to do was get some rest and throw up all the blocks.

I would do this for myself.

And then I'd open the curtains and open the windows and breathe and breathe and breathe.

her mother gives her

---

neither model nor copy

Grace gives Choral a royal blue wool dress she wore
at the bank   a high collar trimmed in matching
lace with darts up the front and back   pulling the
dress tight to her body   sleeves long and tight too
the only alteration she makes is to shorten it to about
mid-thigh   Grace is even skinnier than her   wool
sticks to armpits   wears it first day of school grade
ten indian summer must be near ninety   1969

an enema every night for

---

my clamouring body

from a pile of books in her parents' closet Choral swipes a red-covered *Tropic* book keeps it under her pillow learns the best parts by heart especially the one when the man knocks on the woman's door in the middle of the night and she answers wearing a dressing gown falling loosely open he pulls her close kisses her neck slides his hands inside her gown clasps her breast presses her nipple between his fingers (and she clasps her breast presses her nipple between her fingers) the woman murmurs (and she murmurs) as he picks her up carries her to the bed still groggy half asleep when he enters her (and she licks her fingers so they slide between her legs to the entrance)

that red mouth of mine

in the kitchen Christmas Eve Cora feeds Choral and that boy Arthur's scotch Arthur's beer   pulls that boy close kisses him on the mouth on the teeth their boozy breath   after the music after the dancing Choral and that boy put their coats on put their boots on say we're going for a walk   they get into the back seat of the car in the garage   their hands are cold on their hot skin under their clothes in the dark in the car   scotch and beer on their tongues and lips on necks in ears they struggle with heavy clothes   that boy's fingers fumble with hooks Choral twists to help his hand so warm on her breast   their breathing stopped then faster their mouths and tongues faster and faster Choral's face is hot her head spins   she searches for his zipper his fingers creep past the tops of her nylons run along the edge of her panties   holds her breath   hot wet on her hand that boy moans his fingers find folds of slippery heat

small brown pills every morning until

---

what a mess

Christmas morning Cora disappears   down to the
basement Choral goes to find the presents for Fern
and Ashton   quickly wraps the presents shoves them
under the tree stuffs the turkey puts it in the oven
makes a mincemeat pie   she has watched Cora all
these years   sets the table mashes potatoes carves
the turkey they do not speak of the absence Choral
does not want to think of the night before   the
drinking the fight the screeching   the silence   on
Boxing Day a taxi driver calls Arthur   says he drove
Cora all the way down to Dartmouth in his taxi 250
miles that will be $90 please and later   years
later   Choral laughs and laughs and laughs

she has such bad cramps and

- -

I sew it back together

Choral has such bad cramps deep in her belly below her gut dysmenorrhea they say could be a cyst on her ovaries we'll have to book her for an examination so young almost sixteen just a little ether we'll put her out put her under she'll never know she's so young we'll have to break the hymen Cora warns Choral you'll have to tell that boy he'll never believe you're a virgin if you don't tell him they broke your hymen after the probe the exam (everything looks good) Choral and that boy on the couch in the livingroom breath to breath fear is broken there will be no blood there will be no pain

I was a virgin when I got married

after the second time Cora takes off she returns for her car   when Choral is still a virgin   barely   after the fights two scotch bottles on the windowsill one dark one light   what a dirty trick to water the scotch   after Cora lunges at Arthur with a carving knife   after Arthur smashes Cora into the kitchen door frame popping her ear drum with a hollow snap   blood trickles down the crease of her neck after Cora comes back she announces to Choral it's about time she meets her real father   neither of them mentions her real father is dead from a car crash   and anyway after all these years Choral does not want another parent

she weighs 102 pounds and

---

fold into a being of holes and knots

Arthur dances a little jig sings a little song the baby is born we have a new little girl Choral is sixteen when Cora's last baby is born they name her Leonora Maureen will call her Maureen it's Choral's idea because Eva left it off Leonor's name and because it sounds so much softer Cora decides to add the *a* Eva was always so stupid Leonora Maureen is small only six pounds all pink lots of black fuzzy hair Choral wants to hold the baby so badly wants to hold the baby in her arms but Leonora Maureen stays in the incubator because she can't breathe well no one can hold her and that is the hardest part because Cora had a caesarean had her tubes tied she's confined to the ICU and the baby's confined to the incubator and nobody gets to hold her before she dies *keep me alive and warm*

that Christmas the baby is dead the baby is Cora lies on the couch cold cloth to her face she cannot stand this pain much longer she cannot bear the absence she needs ice from the windows to press to her face she needs dark in the room she needs against the door frame Choral leans attentive accounts for the presents she has bought the kids watches her mother on the couch cold cloth pressed to her face turn the lights off Cora pleads dark and ice are the only relief dark and ice this pain in my face this web in my blue heart

- -

her mother gives her an enema every night for three months and she swallows small brown pills every morning until she has such bad cramps and her shit runs green and she finds she weighs 102 pounds and empties herself no more

SET BACK IN RELATION TO

That Choral, she had a mouth on her.

I don't know why she had to tell everyone Arthur wasn't her real father. If she'd've kept her big mouth shut no one would've ever known. He's not my real father you know. He's not my real father you know. What in the name of god was the matter with her I just don't know, 'cause she accepted him right from the very beginning and he never, ever treated her any differently than the other two.

After all, he chose her when he chose me.

Mouth. That's what I called her. Mouth.

I wouldn't have even brought up the subject of her real father if she'd've kept her big mouth shut. She sure clamped down when I mentioned him. I thought she'd be more interested.

It's hard to know what to tell a child and what to keep quiet.

It's not as if you can ever see a clear path through the string of events you come to regard as your life. Like a net someone throws over you and you pick up the hook and start to add your own stitches. Who knows who cast the first stitches and who this damned thing is supposed to fit. The net grows and grows and grows till one day you look out the corner of your eye and if you squint just right, you can see it has covered everyone. You feel like you're all tangled up and all you can do is roar.

And it's the same damned thing about how you love someone. One day you love them to death and the next day something stupid pops into your head and you can't stand the sight of them.

By the time I took my 250-mile taxi ride, I had had it right up to my throat. And it gets under my skin to think anyone has anything to say about it. It's none of anyone's goddamn business if I want to take a taxi to Dartmouth or to the North Pole for that matter.

I had to get out of there. So I got out for a while but I came back and that's that. Fern wasn't in school yet so I had her sent down to me. The rest of them could just look after themselves. I wasn't gone that long. Five, six weeks. Next time I went was when Arthur broke my ear drum and I had to see the specialist in Dartmouth. Took my car that time and came back when I damned well pleased.

I had my hands full when I got back, didn't I. Got more than my car, didn't I. But I have to say, the prospect of having a sweet warm baby to hold did give me comfort.

And Clarkie. I couldn't just leave Clarkie down there. Poor little bugger. Twenty years old and not much ahead of him. I had to sign papers to get him out of the drug program. I knew he'd be okay with me. He was practically my own child. I couldn't just leave him down there with Eva, she wasn't fit to look after herself let alone someone else. And anyway, she didn't have a clue what was going on outside her own kitchen. That's where her world began and ended. Like with Dad. Her world began and ended with Dad. It was always Orville this and Orville that. Good or bad, it was always about him. Never thought about us. Never thought about her girls. Only her boys, and never thought her boys would give her trouble. Talk about trouble. Christ, that woman never gave me a moment's peace in my life.

When I was down staying with her, she was still snivelling about Grampie Nathaniel dying, for christ's sake. The old bugger was ninety-two years old. Lived a good life. Put in a garden that spring. Same damn thing with Nonnie. You have to tell your mother Nonnie won't make it through the night, Aunt Sophie called to tell me. Poor Eva won't take this very well. You have to be a comfort to your Mumma. Like a fool I sat with her for a couple of hours while she bawled and whined. And I couldn't help but wonder what the hell that was all about. I'll never forget the look on poor little Clarkie's face when I left that night. Get her some pop, was all I could think to tell him. Get her some pop. At least I made sure Nonnie was really dead before I broke the news to her the next time. And didn't the same damned thing happen with Grampie Nathaniel. A couple of times they thought he was gone for sure, but he kept rallying. The doctor said he almost had a heart attack himself when Nathaniel rallied the last time. What a wickedly strong man he was. I thought he was never going to die.

Do you ever think why it takes some people so long to die? You keep wondering what they're waiting for. Then some other people are just gone and all you can say is—what? What. What happened.

But poor old Mumma. Sometimes you had to feel sorry for her. She was simple in the head. Aunt Sophie was always going on about her being so spoiled 'cause she almost died young. Everyone made such a fuss and Grampie Nathaniel bought her that pump organ. But it had to be more. It had to be something more that made her so useless and defenceless.

I never knew what to say. I'd want to ask, Mumma, why do you live like this? Mumma, what's wrong with you? But if a question like that ever raised itself to the tip of your tongue, her eyes would look bigger and her body look smaller till you realized you could never ask such a little person such a big question. It seemed that for a couple of years there was no end to the misery. I felt like such a net of tiredness and sadness and anger had descended on me. And there I was, with nowhere to get away to but poor old Mumma's.

There was never a safe place for a rest. Or time to pull the threads of your balled-up life apart. There was only ever change.

One night Grace got on the phone bawling, what am I going to do, what am I going to do? Christ, I didn't know what I was going to do. All I could think about was when she stayed with us the last time, after Leonor's funeral. She had a purse full of pills, gobbled all the 222s in the house and downed Arthur's scotch. We played musical beds all night. She just wouldn't settle, kept screeching for Mumma to look at her. *Mumma look at me*. Christ, that woman gave me the willies. Then she landed in the kitchen and for god-knows-what reason decided to eat an apple. Said she needed something red. Red. What the hell was that all about. Of course she choked on the apple and I had to stick my fingers down her throat to stop her from choking to death. She wanted to come live with us. Imagine. That was the last thing I needed. I had enough on my hands. I don't care what anyone says. I just couldn't have Grace tripping around here day and night. It was a sad, sad thing that she ended up with Mumma and Dad again but it's not my fault. It's not my fault.

I saw the whole thing happen.

The night Cora had her first car accident was one of those late winter evenings when it's been warm all day and the road freezes up after sunset. We lived next door and I was outside smoking—my husband doesn't let me smoke in the house, can you beat that—well, I saw Cora and Choral get into the car. Cora backed out slowly and started across the road to the bridge. Then swish swish swish she fishtailed and I thought, christ, she's going to hit the bridge. But no, swish swish swish she missed the bridge entirely and plopped right down over the bank. Jesus jesus jesus I yelled but before I could get my boots on, I heard the car door slam and Cora snapping at Choral, what the hell are you snivelling for? Up they crawled over the bank. I stood stock still 'cause I didn't want Cora to see me. Up she marched, like she didn't even see me, right up to their door, yanked it open and barked, Arthur, get off the phone, I just smashed up the car. Choral slithered inside and the front door slammed. I was expecting an explosion or something but no, nothing. It was mighty quiet over there.

When I saw Choral the next day I said, you were some lucky last night. She shot me this sidelong look and said, yeah, we were some lucky alright. You were lucky you both didn't end up in the river, I said. And I could tell I wasn't going to get anything out of her when she answered, we weren't going very fast, Patsy, we got hung up on a tree, that's all. Where were you going, I asked. Out for fries and gravy. Cora wanted to get out for some fries and gravy, she said. Now this might not sound strange to you but it sure as hell did to me. I knew for a fact that Cora was on one of her diets and she had a mind like a steel trap and once she decided to do something, she did it. Fries and gravy my ass.

And anyway, I never ever saw Cora and Choral going anywhere together. I know they spent a lot of time in the house together, especially after the baby died. That was a sad thing, wasn't it. Cora always loved Choral's company, especially when Arthur was busy or away. When she was little, Cora used to let Choral stay up late when Arthur was away and let her sleep with her too. It was awful 'cause Cora kept muttering, stop wriggling around, I can't get to sleep, and the more Cora would say, stop wriggling around, the more Choral'd get itchy and on and on they'd go all night until one of them pooped out and fell asleep. Choral told me herself and she was laughing.

They were a funny bunch. Always someone coming or going. Cora's brother or her sister, and that little friend of Choral's that came to stay off and on for a couple of years. They must have played musical beds or something. And then Cora started disappearing from time to time and nobody ever said a word. Choral just carried on like nothing happened, made all the meals and cleaned up a bit and then Cora would come back and things went back to how they were before.

It's a funny thing about that car accident. Swish bang and it was over. Oh for christ's sake, Patsy, Cora said to me when I asked if she was scared. And you know she damned well wasn't, I could tell by that hard look on her face. It's my guess she'd had a few drinks, that's what. I still can't figure out where they were going. Anyway, it's a good thing the cops weren't called on that one, I'll bet. It was all over town after the second time too, how the cops had taken an illegal blood sample and couldn't use it. But Cora didn't give a shit what people thought by then. And she sure as hell didn't give a shit what I thought, 'though we used to be real good friends. She was the best person you could know, funny and warm, give you the clothes off her backside. Until she'd had a few drinks in her and then she'd turn on you. What wicked things she could say. Of course she'd never remember and you'd never dare mention it.

Come to think of it, she said she was going for french fries the second time too. That's right. She'd been to a baby shower and then decided to go to Bud's up on the highway for some french fries for Ashton 'cause he'd been babysitting Fern all evening. It was raining real hard. Real hard. I wonder where the hell Arthur was.

A CERTAIN BALANCE BETWEEN THE TWO

A couple of months after they moved to Middleton, I came to stay with Choral's family. It seems such an improbable story but when Choral fully understood that I needed a safe place she persuaded Cora to let me come. Cora talked to Arthur and they made room for me. Choral was amazed at how easy it was. But Cora knew what it was like to live with a drunken slobbering father. They didn't ask my family for room and board money, they only asked that I buy my own clothes and school supplies and have some spending money.

Choral moved a cot into her room and put the heads of our beds end-to-end. My first night we slept holding hands across our pillows. After a while we talked Ashton into giving up his bed for the cot and we set up the twin beds on opposite walls. Sometimes we traded the twin beds with Choral's parents for their double bed, depending on how well they were sleeping.

Of course my spending money didn't arrive on a regular basis so Choral shared her allowance. When Cora ordered Choral a pair of brown leather boots with a snazzy buckle from the catalogue, it was more than evident that I desperately wanted a pair too. Cora ordered the same ones for me with the promise that my brother would pay her back. This was the bargain we made so I could save face.

They had moved to Middleton so Arthur could start his own business. Cora worked afternoons in the store. They never knew from one week to the next how things were going to be. Sometimes there was good money and sometimes there was just enough.

Those identical leather boots helped Choral and I to act out the story we told everyone about being real sisters. They hadn't lived in Middleton long enough for most people to know. There were only six months between us and we were able to play the line quite well because she was in grade nine and I was in grade ten.

We were on the tear all the time, more goofy than troublesome. We more or less let Cora know where we were and let ourselves into the house at a decent hour, quiet as church mice. No curfews. We were expected to be good.

On our walks home, we blasted the dead quiet of midnight singing *Creeque Alley* or practised songs from *Down in the Valley*, our school's operetta. When we'd really get going, we'd move right out into the middle of the road and change the words to old songs, like *how I love to feel your organ behind the chapel in the moonlight*. But when we got close to the house, the main thing was to not wake up Arthur. He didn't like to have his sleep disturbed.

The next day Cora was always waiting to hear the details of our escapades and we pretty well always told the truth. We used to make things up to shock her and she'd only laugh at us and get us to tell more. So we'd think up something outrageous, bug our eyes out and say we'd been out grassin', or out shaggin' around. One time when Cora said she didn't believe a word we said, Choral tried out *well fuck you, Mom*, and Cora just came right back with *well fuck you too, dear*. That shut Choral right up. I could tell by the look on her face how shocked she was to hear her mother say such a dirty word. Oh you girls, Cora said. What you haven't figured out yet is that if you've got *it*, you don't talk about *it*.

After we'd finished the supper dishes we'd make Cora a cup of tea and sit around in the kitchen. Sometimes we'd set her hair in rollers and tease it up into a parody of the popular styles. Cora even let

Choral cut her hair with one of Arthur's razors. One time Choral got one of those streaking kits and Cora put it in for her. What a holy mess. She looked like a raccoon. Cora had to get money from Arthur to send her off to the hairdressers for a fix-up.

There was always a cigarette lit in the ashtray. We'd sneak drags behind her back but she must have known because we'd give ourselves away with giggles.

Whatever was going on in that house between the parents, we didn't discuss. All our talk was reserved for boys. Even when Cora would take off from time to time, we didn't talk about it. The worst was the Christmas morning she disappeared. I went to my sister's place for the holidays and when I got back Choral's mouth was swollen shut with a mass of cold sores. For three or four days she could only drink cold fluids from a straw.

We were both cheerleaders. Choral was the co-captain and went to the student council and talked them into giving us money for new uniforms. The basketball team was mad as all-get-out because they wanted new uniforms too, but there was only so much money and she won out. Which was typical of Choral, because once she made up her mind to do something, she usually got her way. Well, new uniforms turned out to be only material and patterns. We were expected to have our mothers sew them up. Choral would never mention that her mother wasn't home, so we dragged out Cora's old sewing machine. We pieced and patched, got them to stay together and though they didn't quite match up to everyone else's, they were good enough. We were very proud.

Cora was away a lot the second year I lived there. When she came back five months pregnant, with Clarkie in tow, there was no more room for me. One afternoon before I left, Cora came into the room with a pile of clean laundry. Choral was watching for a friend out the window and I was stretched out across my bed.

Geeze I'd sure love to have a cigarette, I sighed, yawning and eyeballing Cora. She put the clean clothes down, never missed a beat. Well, Reowna, why don't you ask Choral for one, she suggested, smoothing out the creases I had made on the bedspread. She's got a whole pack of Rothman's in her top drawer.

she cuts her hair with

---

my sorrow and rage

rain rain rain for eighteen hours campers in wet clothes wait in line   comfort bawling babies Choral heaves trays pours coffee balances plates of bacon and eggs toast sliding to the floor in the kitchen   the owner rests her hand on Choral's arm get your coat dear   Choral notices her soon-to-be-mother-in-law standing by the door trying to arrange her face   fans of needles shoot through Choral's limbs over her skin into her gut as she floats over the floor to her soon-to-be-mother-in-law   there's been an accident   she directs Choral into the waiting car   your mother was in a car crash just after midnight

---

neither speech nor death

standing at her bedside Choral looks at Cora's bloody head   this face does not look like the face of her mother   there is an inventory of body parts they say are damaged   body parts that are bound body parts that are hoisted   chained to contraptions   pelvis is smashed the left knee has chunks missing   right arm is broken   several ribs are cracked at least three vertebrae are crushed   internal bleeding   neck and head injuries   glass in her hair face embedded in her back and knee   they can't give her pain killers because of the concussion don't know if she'll live   her head full of glass it's certain she won't walk again   Choral cannot grasp her mother's body but knows her voice hears her speak   am I going to die Cora asks   *no Mommy no Mommy*   she cannot stand this pain much longer   Cora pleads I hope I die I hope I die from the cabinet and he complains

---

oh mercy me I laugh and laugh

the day of Choral's wedding Cora gets out of traction they let her out of the hospital for Choral's wedding she comes to the church on a hospital stretcher covered in eggshell blue satin wearing an eggshell blue lacy negligee they slit down the back and drape around her Choral always laughs at the wedding picture outside the anglican church everyone standing at the head of the stretcher where Cora's all decked out big smiley face Ashton and Clarkie kneeling on either side but the first thing noticed the first thing noticed are the shiny bottoms of Cora's new white high heels pointing straight to heaven *never believe it*

before Cora gets out of the hospital Arthur presents her with an itemized list of how much she has cost him over the years   years later he tells Choral he is not proud of some of the things he has done   Cora would never believe it   they say she will never walk again   that Christmas Choral can't believe Cora could clean the carpets   Cora laughs that even with one leg longer than the other she can still get around   nothing can stop her now   nothing can shut her up   at the dinner table Choral is silenced when Cora is drunk   stammers that that other boy is still in love with her   holiday times and all the other times she just won't shut up   Choral keeps a snapshot of that Christmas   Arthur's arm across Cora's shoulder Fern at their side all eyes straight ahead stiff   Cora is so skinny she has no breasts

----

she cuts her hair with her father's razor blades from the cabinet and he complains when they are missing or dull

When Cora announced it was time to meet my real father and asked if I wanted to see him, I didn't have an answer. What could I say? After a while I reasoned that maybe he'd buy me a leather jacket. And then I felt ashamed. Even at sixteen, I knew a leather jacket was a poor excuse to meet a real father.

Perhaps it was shock. How did he surface, I wondered but was too stunned to ask. And why have you surrendered the dead father and the car accident and the tragic widow, I wondered. At least when he was dead I never had to imagine him face-to-face. I never wondered what he looked like. He looked like death. Void. Blank. A cancelled cheque. And now he'd bounced back after all these years. What was I supposed to do? Cash him in?

My real dead father was resurrected and immediately I felt ashamed. What could I ever possibly have to say to him? What was I supposed to call him? A real dead father isn't Dad. I have a Dad. Arthur. Cora gave him to me. He didn't give me to her.

In the end we didn't revive him. Which was a big relief to me. I had no words for an absent father.

It was hard enough to find the words for the present one.

Before my wedding, when Cora was still in intensive care, I needed something useful to do, something to restore order in that household before I left it for good. I scrubbed out the fridge, emptied and cleaned the cupboards, was down on my hands and knees scraping out the oven when Arthur came galloping through the front door and rushed right up to me, his face an intense worried wobble.

I've just been talking to one of the doctors who came to see your mother, he began, his black beard twitching. He said to ask you if the only reason you're getting married is to get out of the house. Are you only getting married to get out of the house?

I watched him for a moment, his long body suspended over me like a huge question mark. He wasn't breathing. I could blow on him and he'd topple over.

No, Dad, I answered calmly.

Good, he breathed. Good. I had to ask. And as abruptly as he had approached, he left.

It was the first question he had ever asked me.

After Jay and I started going together, Cora called me into her room one evening. With no preamble she just flat out put it to me: Are you and Jay sleeping together? Yes. But it's okay Mom, I'm on the pill. She was folding sheets and her arms froze straight out at her sides. The sheet hung suspended between us. She blinked and blinked and blinked as if she had mechanical eyes. Didn't you want to be a virgin on your wedding night? No, I answered, clamping down hard on the temptation to inform her I wasn't even a virgin when I met Jay. But you're only seventeen, she said more to herself than to me.

She had missed the big event. She had missed the deep grooves of my relationship with that other boy and our love-making, my bare bum shoved up against her bread box in the kitchen. She had missed my broken heart when that other boy told me he didn't love me anymore.

Cora couldn't stand the idea of me going to the drugstore for my birth-control pills, so she picked them up. It was impossible to argue with her. I knew she only wanted me to have a life different from hers. But I had been watching, listening all those years. I was learning to make choices, to move about quietly. To practise questions instead of being at the mercy of bad answers.

I didn't know how long it would take.

And the first thing I practised was tucking my real dead father back into the nether world, where he belonged.

the difference between pleasure and pain

for the last time   when Orville comes home off the boat he settles back in with Eva   Cora won't go down there to stay anymore   not even when she and Arthur separate again   not even to help with Eva's legs   well you can say one thing about him Cora concedes   he always sent Eva just enough money   the last time Choral saw Orville he was grey all over   skin hair eyes   brought her a bag of penny candy now he can't believe she's married no one can believe he's back   oh Eva I always loved you so much he lurched at her one night falling down dead drunk across her dead legs   so brittle they snap snap osteoporosis the doctor said Leonor never believed she had a real medical problem   misuse she claimed   but gangrene is real enough   the green and purple splotches her wrists with razor blades and the doctor tells

---

the irruption within the order

the second-last time Cora and Arthur split up she
moves back to Shipton where she hasn't lived for
twenty years   Choral and Jay borrow Arthur's van
to pick up Cora's furniture but Choral doesn't tell
Arthur she may be moving the furniture somewhere
else   so Cora can be reunited with Choral's real
dead father   who has tracked her down after all
these years   Choral arrives in Shipton waits at
Aunt Sophie's for Cora's instructions   feels sick
wants to throw up sits on the wine plush sofa forever
in her livingroom   waits for the click of Cora's
longer leg   Aunt Sophie says listen dear I hate to
tell you this but you should know   I hate to tell
you this but your mother slit her wrists used a razor
slit her wrists before she moved back here   Fern
found her in the kitchen sharpening a knife   it
slipped she said

her if she is really serious about this

---

peg me to the bed

by the time Choral gives birth to Juel great-grandmother Eva and great-grandfather Orville live in a dingy two-bedroom apartment in a square brick block Eva keeps her bed in the livingroom with the TV because she already has one leg cut off Grace is back from Toronto her hair still shoulder length the brown curtains are always closed and the lights always on because you never know when Eva might need the bedpan Orville get me the pan or get me some pop or get me the ashtray they smoke day and night Orville cooks steaks and onions with boiled potatoes and canned peas in her floral shiny gowns Grace lies on the couch the TV is on twenty-four hours a day above it hangs an ornamental tray Orville brought back from a trip to the Orient overlapping blue and gold butterflies behind plate glass

she should slit her wrists

---

right up into my throat

for years and years Grace stows her body with pills and booze then pukes and pukes   her heart gets so bad the same doctors who wrote all those prescriptions and held her skinny hand   open her up and put in a shiny new pacemaker   she comes back to live with Eva and Orville   she comes back to die on the couch in the front room where her one-legged mother spends her days and nights   she simply died the doctor says she lost the will to live Choral wonders what happened to Grace's favourite cat Patchy

stop screeching

Cora buys a new cape and soft hat to wear to Grace's funeral travels alone on the train stays at Choral's apartment she lives close by Eva now to keep Eva company Choral goes over with Juel promises to come back and give her a perm some day feels bad because she could do more for her poor old grandmother but can't figure out exactly what this would be thinking about her two dead daughters Eva cries a little nobody knows nobody knows she tut-tuts can't go to the funeral because she needs to get her other leg cut off soon Choral can't go because she has to keep Eva company

I'm just resting my eyes

after Cora leaves Arthur for good   stays with
Choral for a while gets a part-time job so she can
afford a few things   makes plans contacts old allies
Choral will not speak to her real dead father when
he calls   so she can get out once in a while Cora
babysits for Choral which is more than Cora could
ever expect from that bunch she came from   after
a party Choral can't sleep is so tired the next day
Cora says take a nap take one of these little pills
won't hurt you I take them all the time   that
evening at supper Choral flops flat out in her plate
almost three days before she can function speak
without her lips in the way   after Cora leaves to
start her new life Choral and Jay clean her room
find empty vodka bottles under the mattress and in
the hamper   so that's why all the orange juice
disappeared

---

she slits her wrists with razor blades and the doctor tells her if she is really serious about this she should slit her wrists vertically not horizontally, then hold them under warm water

Cora told me she had an operation on her wrists to fix the tendons. I didn't ask too much, I was immune to the details of her mutilations. Especially after the car accident. Totally conscious through the crash, trapped in the car, the pain afterwards. The crippling effects on her body and soul completely possessed her. Her speech was littered with these events. How could anyone bear so much pain?

So I sat in Aunt Sophie's living room, cushioning her tattle about Cora's wrist-slitting with my ten-week-old baby. Juel was my focus. She was difficult and I attended to her every whimper. I didn't want to think about the torment that led Cora to such a mean and hard decision. I didn't want to think about Fern finding her. The blood. The desperation.

I tried to shut out Aunt Sophie's story but I could no more plug my ears than I could plug the pores of my skin. My very pores were listening. Every word she spoke was absorbed and stored away in my flesh.

I was hoping Aunt Sophie could provide me with a kinder prattle as I cradled my baby and awaited Cora's instructions about her furniture and future. Maybe Aunt Sophie didn't know about Cora's dilemma. That's hard to believe since Sophie's the one who told my real dead father that Cora was back in town, living alone with her two younger children. It was Aunt Sophie who showed him snapshots from my childhood, off and on through the years. He even had photographs from my wedding. And now, disentangled from his wife, he had presented himself to Cora.

I tried to picture what Cora was up to. Above all I wanted her to find some happiness. I seriously doubted her return to Arthur was anything more than a temporary measure. But I also didn't believe she could recover her former lover.

Perhaps Aunt Sophie didn't notice I wasn't feeling well, that I couldn't eat, that I couldn't respond to her tut-tut tales. How could she have guessed I was confounded by the two possibilities fighting in my chest? What will I say to my real dead father if we take Cora's furniture to his place? What will I say to Arthur?

How could Cora put me in such a predicament?

How did I get there so quietly?

Was it the noise of her pain that held me witness?

Why the hell would anyone be interested in me being in love with Jimmy McNeil. That was too long ago to be worth thinking about. And whether or not I married Hank Norton and what our marriage was like is none of anyone's goddamn business. Who could possibly know what my life was like. Or care for that matter.

I did okay considering that bunch I had to put up with. That cracked-ass father of mine and a mother you couldn't keep track of. One minute blubbering over Orville and the next sneaking out the bedroom window to meet her own Jimmy. Another catholic. But I guess a secret catholic lover doesn't matter. Not like she was going to marry him or anything. Just a little company while her own true love's off fighting the war or sailing around the world on an oil tanker. Talk about a tailspin.

My clock conked out. So what. Have you got a more divine schedule than me. Do you want to talk to me about hanging in there. Shit. I hung in there. But how long is good enough. How long would make you satisfied. Till I made full manager at the bank. Till I brought another bundle of joy into this stinking world. Why should I work eighty hours a week to satisfy someone else's schedule of success. Why should I keep my ovaries soft and plump with the blood flowing. To bring another little girl into this family. Christ. And don't you worry. I would have squeezed out a boy before he even took hold. I never even liked kids. Can't anyone ever get that through their thick heads. I never wanted kids. There's nothing wrong with that.

I had more than my fair share of a mother-daughter relationship.

There was no way I wanted to live through that again, even if it meant being on the powerful end. It makes me weary to think about it.

I was the oldest and Mumma never let me forget it. All the time, she used me as a shield from that great big husband of hers. And it was me who had to clean her up after their brawls. Wipe the blood off her mouth, get some ice for her bruises. And not once, not once did she ever do anything special for me. Never even acknowledged my success at the bank.

Cora and Leonor went away to Nonnie and Grampie Nathaniel's all the time but I had to stay with Mumma. She wouldn't let me go down to Ecum Secum unless she was going too, which wasn't very often 'cause she hated it down there. By the time Dad went away to the war I felt like we were stitched together. If she even got a scratch on her, I felt guilty. Then Junior was born and he filled her life like Dad had always filled her, but she had control of Junior. She made a fool out of that kid. So with Dad gone and a baby to occupy her, she only needed me to look after the house. I was still the prisoner, only not in such a privileged position. From personal bodyguard and nurse to chief cook and bottle-washer, I was demoted by the time I was ten.

I was in my thirties before I finally understood that her miserableness was not my fault. That I would never be able to save her. None of us could save her. That damned woman wouldn't let me out of her sight. She couldn't stand Leonor. And Cora got squeezed right up the middle.

To tell the truth, I'm at a loss to explain why I married Hank Norton. I might have got by okay if I had just stayed in Toronto alone. I could have worked on making myself into a well and happier person if I wasn't so damned mixed up with a drunk just like Dad. Hank wasn't such a bad man. It's just that we made such a sorry couple. We each needed too much. And we did try in the beginning to act like what we thought was normal people. Like the people I saw in my bank every day, crawling on their bellies for a loan just so they can look okay to the world and have all the right things. Be all the right things. A nice little family with a nice little house and car and a goddamn dog. I didn't believe that pile of crap. I didn't believe in anything.

How many times do you have to be beat over the head before you realize it doesn't matter. It just doesn't matter. And I'm not talking *all you need is love* crap either. All you need is to get to the next day. When you get to the point that the next day utterly doesn't matter, what business is it of anyone's. What makes anyone think they could set my timer. It's not as if I came with a warranty.

When Leonor died and we made that trip down to see Mumma, I was overcome with grief. Grief at the stupidity of her death and the waste of a life not really ever started. But I realized I was really grieving for myself. I saw that until the moment she died, I always thought everything would turn out okay. If a warm and loving woman like Leonor had lost the chance to make some kind of peaceful existence for herself, I knew I'd lost my chance too.

Hell, lost it. Never even had it.

I knew what kind of schedule I was on. What good would old age have done me anyhow. Starving is not my idea of the twilight years. All those years I practised being hungry. I knew I didn't want to spend my old age like that. Suffering. Who would suffer a skinny old starving woman. Starving for food, starving for affection, let's name it, starving for love. Oh yeah, like I wanted to end my days like that.

About a year after Leonor's funeral I called Cora, made one last whiney appeal. Cried to her that I wanted to come live with her. But what could she do with three kids and that foolish Clarkie, another one of Mumma's screw-ups. And pregnant. At her age. Did she think she could replace Leonor or something?

If that Grace was here right now I'd plow her into next week. God, it gets right up into my throat. Suffer my ass. She suffered if she had to change the toilet paper roll. Leonor was a lovely person, always laughing. A warm, warm person. And all her warmth went into her children and everyone she knew. I wish I could've been like her. How could anyone replace Leonor? Shows you Grace never knew a goddamn thing. Everybody loved Leonor except Mumma and that's why Leonor always lived down in Ecum Secum with Nonnie and Grampie Nathaniel when she was little.

I can't even talk about it.

When I married Arthur, Leonor made all the arrangements for the reception. Couldn't afford a dress to stand up with me, but she made a little yellow dress for Choral to wear afterwards at the house. I didn't let her go to the church. It didn't seem right. She stayed at Mumma's to keep her company.

Grace could afford the matron of honour's dress alright and there she is in the wedding pictures. Right beside me with her skinny little arms and neck. Jesus, she was so thin you could see her ovaries. *She* could afford a dress. *She* worked in a bank. *She* made everyone jump through hoops for *my* wedding, then she and Eva got into it. Drunk and fighting. Christ, it just never stopped.

One time I didn't see Leonor for a while and then she showed up with her hair dyed black. Said, you always had dark hair and now I've got dark hair.

We were always carrying on. Nonnie and Grampie Nathaniel came up to Shipton one weekend to stay with Aunt Sophie. Leonor and Archie and their second baby, Jeff, were down in Ecum Secum alone. I was about three months pregnant with Choral, feeling pretty lonely, so I got her father to drive me down there. We got carrying on and laughing. Wouldn't it be fun to send out for chicken? Imagine. Down there in the middle of nowhere. That Archie, he said he could get some chicken at Reverend Tufts'. Oh what a handsome devil that Reverend was, six-foot-four. I had such a crush on him the year I was fourteen. He had a real nice wife and five little boys. Bang. Bang. Bang. Bang. Bang. Kept prize roosters. Pure white. Well, Archie and Choral's father went off, cock-sure and full of the devil, and grabbed two roosters. Brought them back to Nathaniel's and killed them and cooked them. When Reverend Tufts came by the next day to get his milk—he always got his milk from Nathaniel—I was sitting on the couch with Jeff. Couldn't even look at him. He never would have suspected us, poor man. His prize roosters, he never said a word.

Poor, poor, poor soul. There was something evil between Leonor and Mumma. Mumma even told Archie the only child of his was Jeff. Started saying that awful evil thing when Gail was born. Leonor got her revenge. Wrote a nasty letter to Eva and read it right out loud in front of everyone. About her having a heart of stone, how she would turn to stone all over and her beautiful fingers would fall off one by one and then her right leg and her left leg, and finally those great big poppy eyes would scale over and turn to rock right there in her head. Imagine. Leonor never lived to see it. The things they did to each other.

That hard look on Mumma's face.

I lift from the slit of my life

after the last time Cora leaves finally Choral is pregnant again she takes her little girl Juel to visit Arthur he asks her to clean out some bedroom drawers Cora left in such a hurry didn't even take everything with a couple of big green garbage bags Choral sits on his bed bends over the bureau fills the bags from the back of a drawer she picks up a porcelain box pink with real gold trim a porcelain box pink with real gold trim that she doesn't know Cora keeps at the back of a drawer lifting the lid Choral quickens to see little white shards can't be bones can't be bones just the coffin the little white baby coffin but the grey powder has to be powdered bones powdered bones and little white shards in the porcelain box pink tucked away in the back of a drawer in a bureau all by herself Leonora Maureen

I sprawl everywhere so stretched

to start labour the midwife gives Choral castor oil
makes her shit and vomit at the same time   sticks
her in a damned hot bath her contractions start
then stop   too bad   midwife hoped to avoid the
drip   Choral gets hooked   after twenty-four
hours of labour given a rest for the night   pains
keep coming today is Leonora Maureen's eighth
birthday Choral is not superstitious   they keep her
on the drip   at night her water finally breaks contractions really strong now   doctor gives her a shot
don't give me Demerol it makes me vomit   he
laughs and she vomits half an hour later green bile
from so deep thinks she'll throw her insides out
Choral is not dilating can't stand this pain much
longer   suddenly suddenly Choral has to bear
down the baby is coming midwife cuts her vagina
so stretched it snaps snap a baby wooshes into life
doctor lifts baby up up she cries chokes stops
sputters   he rushes from the room with baby Jay
behind   midwife kneads Choral's belly whispers
breathe my beauty breathe my beauty breathe   not
superstitious at all they name her Belle she is pink
with dark fuzzy hair and she breathes

out the doctor asks will you

---

stand this pain much longer

Choral travels with her girls to visit Eva great-grandmother with the cut-off legs bedridden in the nursing home they bring her an azalea she is so harmless now a well-meaning cousin drags Choral into the men's unit your poor grandfather he always loved you so much on his left side fetal position lies Orville striped pyjamas that hold no body just skin stretched skull enormous hands look Orville it's Choral she came to see you he opens his eyes she says hello and even if it is true that Eva wouldn't let Cora keep her and Orville comes home from the boat says where's the baby and Cora screeches Eva won't let me keep her and he bellows why the hell not calls a taxi they go to the hospital to get Choral back even if it is true it has nothing to do with the man in the bed still think of yourself as a woman

---

(I am) my real father

in a final attempt   to make contact Choral's real
dead father arranges to pick up Cora at Choral's
home where she is visiting   they are going out for
dinner   Choral will not move from her spot on the
couch with her back to the hall she hears him at the
door   nor will she greet him on the phone when
he calls for Cora a few years later   and many years
later Choral realizes he is old   perhaps he has
something to say she should try to make contact
Cora cannot find him   he is angry   he thinks she
has kept him away from Choral for all these years

---

hold me witness

years later Cora phones Choral at Christmas to accuse and blame   relentless   Choral hangs up she won't stop she just won't stop her voice pulling through the wires squeezing through the wires (smashed the pretty ornament)   you don't know what they've done to me you don't know what they've done to me all these years Cora cries   (sharp sharp edges)   that's the difference between us (edges to slice through)   you don't know what they've done to me and now you don't care you just don't care you've got everything you want now (under the tree in a hundred pieces)   that's the difference between us   you've got everything and I've got nothing   (shiny fragments reflecting light) must hang up even if she slits her wrists again   Choral chooses   (red and gold blue and veined)   I'm going to finish decorating the tree *this web in my blue heart*

to reduce the puffiness from crying hard   Choral holds an ice-bag to her face she had too much to drink last night   she knows better than this she has seen the damage it's in her skin her blood a dangerous inheritance   it can only make you sad   too much booze too much grief I have to guard myself watch every day Choral tenderly reminds herself

----

before she gets her uterus cut out the doctor asks
will you still think of yourself as a woman if you
don't bleed every month

Sometimes I look in the mirror and say, well Cora, why are you still alive.

My sixtieth birthday. I could have left this one behind. I didn't mind thirty, I didn't mind forty or even fifty. But I've got to say, this one is bad. I figure I've got fifteen years. Mumma was seventy-six and Dad seventy-five. So I figure I've got about fifteen years to do something.

And now Junior's gone. Fifty-two. It's amazing he lived this long. Poor little bugger. It seems so sad to die all alone in your sleep. Heart failure. I feel right bad about him dying all alone. I feel right bad 'cause I wouldn't let anyone tell him where I was after I got married again. I just couldn't have him around here on one of his binges, full of crazy schemes that always meant someone had to bail him out. Drunk and crying and feeling sorry for himself. There is no way to approach the self-pity of a drunk.

He was a grown man before they stopped calling him Junior. No matter what he was up to, he always landed on his feet. But he took a lot of people down with him along the way. Like that first sweet little wife of his and those two sweet kids. One night they landed at our place after a great big fight. He was on a bender. She just didn't know what to do. I called her father and told him if he cared anything at all about his daughter, he should come get her and never let her go back.

I wish someone would have done that for Mumma. I wish Grampie Nathaniel could have got off his belligerent high horse long enough to be of some use. The self-righteous old bastard.

But no matter what Junior did, he always owned up to it. And he never said anything to anyone else about what they did or didn't do. Not like that Clarkie. Sticking his finger under my nose and Mumma's nose when Grace died. As if there was anything we could do about the way she lived. Who the hell did he think he was. And now we can't even find him to tell him Junior's dead.

I guess he got out for good.

All you can do is go on, I guess. I'm never going to give in. It's like the doctor said, you're going to die of either cancer or a heart attack. Maybe cancer would be better, like Dad. They have so many good drugs they can give you today. Try to make it painless. That way it would be slower, you'd have time to say some things to some people. I don't like to think about a sudden hard pain in my chest up to my throat, wanting to say hey, just a minute, I'm not finished yet, there are some things that I haven't said yet.

These people who were my parents. They always wanted you close by and you wanted to be there but you couldn't stand it. Even though they're dead it's still hard to find a place safe from them. I hope we aren't in the same place after I die.

How do you tell a person you love to stop stop stop I can't stand the pain in your life much longer. Do you have to wait till you stop loving. Do you have to take the pain 'cause you're attached. And after a while, how can you tell the difference between loving a person and living their pain.

When I was sixteen I started to teach Sunday School. Mumma never stepped inside a church after she left Ecum Secum except to go to funerals and by the time Junior was born she never even did that anymore. I went to church all by myself. It was peaceful there. I wish I could have found that again.

I know I'm not like Mumma and Dad. I don't know if it's hereditary or what, but every day of my life I fought to stay sane. My sanity was not a present at birth. I have to guard it. Grace could always look after herself and Leonor couldn't. That was the difference between them.

Leonor made my confirmation dress. She understood the church was a safe and quiet place for me. It's only lately I can go to bed at night and not see her face in the casket. It's the worst thing I ever saw in my life.

Look, so what if I took a few drinks now and then. What goddamn business is it of anyone's. Christ, all I ever had was a pint of vodka once a week. That's all I ever could afford. What business is it of anyone's.

You can't control another person's life. We never could do anything about Dad, but I went to the nursing home as often as I could when he was dying. He was always such a big handsome man and there he was all shrivelled up on a hard white bed in a comfortless place. Sometimes I wished I could just tie him up and tell him what he'd done, but of course I couldn't. The old recreant. That man was so strong, a week before he died he walked out to the nurses' station with his supper tray. The doctor told me he'd given him enough drugs to fell an elephant.

That's the best way. Let them knock you out. Then you're not struggling.

When Mumma was dying I told the doctor, when she comes out of one dose of morphine I want you to give her another dose. Don't let her suffer anymore. She couldn't even see. Cataracts. Eyes like stone. I knew what she was like all her life, but I was there when she died. Her heart got her in the end.

I held her hands, her beautiful cold hands, and had my arm around her shoulder when she took her last breath. I'm glad I was there.

Mouth.

It was never about the mouth or the father.

It was about the mothers and the birthings and the secrets.

The real father isn't the story. The father isn't the real story. It's the balled-up story of mothers and daughters and sisters and aunts. It wasn't the father's name I wanted, but a whole story I could mouth. But your mouth was a mouth wide open full of Mumma Nonnie Leonor Grace Cora Cora. Cora's got her teeth again teeth again teeth again teeth again. Cora, why can't you swipe that stupid song and bite a hunk of peace for yourself instead of that nameless, useless rage and screech? I needed speech beyond screech. Speech and a script I was part of, not witness to.

I was always aware of your grief. You could have shared it, but you thought you protected me. Telling lies, excuses. Keeping me away from funerals. You could have told it all. The whole thing. Not just the bits and pieces I heard, the bits and pieces I saw. The in-between spaces I can't fill in. The in-between spaces pool around me. Amniotic lies flood me. Did you think the presence of your body between me and the whole bloody story provided protection? Did you think I wouldn't absorb all the noise of your rage, your grief?

Like a little sponge I soaked it all up. I'm going to squeeze myself out now. I'm going to wring all the bad dreams out.

You think I never grieved the loss of Leonor and her warm breathy embrace, her funny stories. Her plots for escape from the forces she kept edging and ducking like sudden snowstorms out of nowhere.

I was grieving but you never asked me. As if it didn't matter that I loved her too.

The birthing and the dying. The bits and pieces of all the mothers and daughters in between. Grace in her grisly bone-sucked skin. She got away, but not for long or safe enough to escape. Only long enough for no one to mourn her. And what about Leonora, baby girl. Did she escape?

There are pools of truth. Floods of indiscretion.

Eva, Eva what happened to your legs?

Was a line sent out?

To the difference between us.

My hands are still cold.

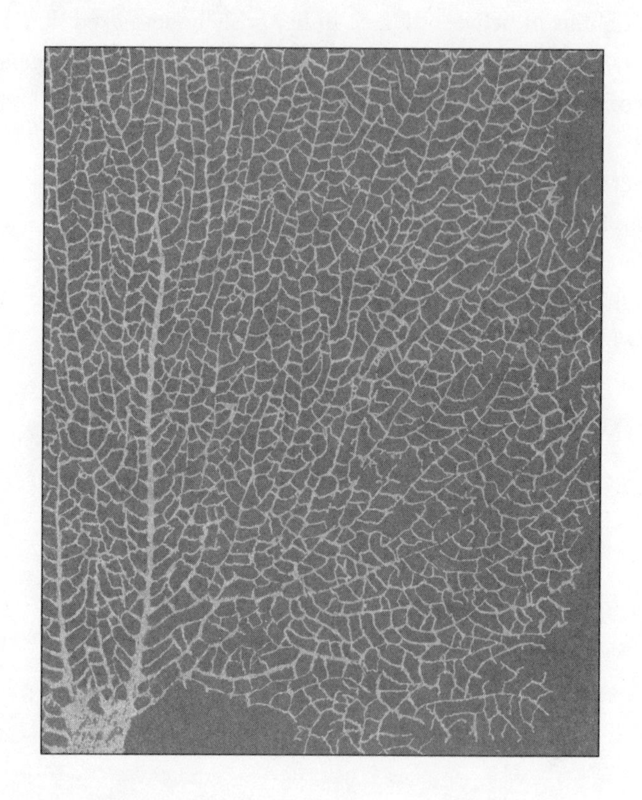

I was lifted through a slit in my mother's anesthetized body. I was lifted from the warm water of my mother's belly. Never did I catch my breath. Never did I learn to breathe out of the sloshy surround of warm water. I was lifted from the small slit of my life. Lifted from the story, almost. Leonora Maureen. Such a long and complicated name for such a short, uncomplicated life. *The baby*, they call me. But it's not very often they call me.

I heard what you were thinking. I heard what nobody said. Perhaps it's a small mercy. She's better off. Better off not knowing, not having to live through all that mess. What were her chances, really.

Don't talk to me about chances. I might have had a little life but I had plans. Big plans.

Don't talk to me about mercy.

Mercy me.

Mercy my.

Anyway, it's not so bad tucked away down here with Nonnie. I'm glad Cora finally found a place for me. Nonnie's old rotting bones and my baby powdered bones. Covered together. We're getting to know each other, there's a lot to catch up on. We're making plans, punching out, parading the future with big-mouthed women who know who to talk to.

We don't think too much of doctors. Not since we got the short end of a very long and very crooked stick. Pill-pushers, flesh-invaders, careless and neglectful SOBs, Nonnie says. She still can't swear right out but she's learning. Says too many of those white-cloaked men have the same affliction as Nathaniel. They should listen instead of poke poke poking a body, plugging you up with pills and potions. I'm not sure what she means, but she says I'll get it soon enough. Know-it-all-bastards, she finally squirts out and I giggle away. Think they have the right to poke and plug, practise and practise on a person's body as if it didn't belong to anyone in particular. Listening only to their own smug pronouncements. Ha!

We don't have to mind our manners tucked away down here in the cold earth. We don't have to hush and worry about being respectful of our betters. There's nobody better than us down here. We're not mean. Not at all. We just talk about things the way we know them.

Feels rate good, Nonnie says. Feels rate good to speak up. Should have spoken up a hundred years ago. And then she laughs and laughs.

Oh mercy us we laugh and laugh.

And I wonder, Cora, are my eyes like yours. Would their blue follow you around the room. Does my hair curl. Is it soft and dark. Do I grit my teeth when I think of holding you, like you grit your teeth when you love so hard. Is my face round. Body plump. Do I clench my hands and tap my fingers when I say one thing and mean another. And do I smile or laugh or care too much, my warm lips pulsing over perfect white teeth. Are my eyes like yours.

Do I sing like you.

We like to dance. Nonnie and me. The jigs and the reels of time flying by. We've got all the time in the world. It feels rate good to have you here for company, Nonnie tells me. Even though Nathaniel's just over there. We don't disturb him. He's still the deaf one.

As for me, I'm rate glad to keep Nonnie company. But I can't help but wonder what promise I held.

Choral journeys through fractures

---

behind me and in front of me

can't find it either Cora tells Choral   driving down the Eastern Shore haven't been as far as Ecum Secum for thirty years   can't find it either and Choral is stranded by the notion Cora can't find the place where she squirted milk from cows' udders into the mouths of mewley kittens and Nonnie made her foxberry pies   where she learned to skin a rabbit and Eva's rages couldn't touch her   down and back up narrow dirt lanes they drive over the rocky landscape rocky crawling with orange lichen and the rustle of snakes through the blueberry bushes and the fat sweet blueberries   blackflies that suck tender necks and hair pulled tight in braids so the bloody blackfly trails won't cake in dark brown hair   rocks rocks rocks and more rocks and the big flat rock where Nonnie and Nathaniel built their house *throw out the dregs*

down in Ecum Secum the mighty summer storms rolling boiling nights of rain and lightning and thunder rattling loose window panes of slumped glass distorting every flash of light on the branches that scrape the surface of imagination of Uncle Stanley in his closed-up room of the baby crying with holes in his heart of a hollow clink clink that could be a song or fingers stroking silent keys or good white teeth falling out one by one of Nonnie stricken on the porch teapot in hand or lying in the bed downstairs with her breasts cut off of Nathaniel lying next to her too deaf to hear the storm

an idealized misconception

all that summer Choral tells Cora she is terrified of what Cora asks of ghosts of lightning and thunder of witches who could cast a spell on anyone witches Cora asks witches did you ever hear fingers clink to the ground and Choral laughs asks have you got new teeth your teeth are different not so comfortable these new teeth and Choral starts to hum a little tune *lada da da dadada dadada* what Cora asks what as Choral wavers off into a flat tuneless hum sometimes I have bad dreams about my teeth falling out what would you have bad dreams for Cora can't imagine

I'm not struggling

Choral peels the sock off her left foot looking for a place of harvest   the right foot has a limited yield only a flake on the big toe   little toe is punctuated with a dot of blood from the night before   I'm getting a little squeamish about foot-peeling she says to herself   thirty years ago I didn't flinch at bloody heels   carefully she inserts her thumb and index finger under the envelope of hard skin plying it back and forth until a thin strip can be pulled from the resistance of living flesh   flesh flagrant petals oh tiny morsels

---

now

into the mirror Choral asks why are these bad dreams still alive   a three-sided mirror where she can perceive herself and herself and herself   turn a stage then another stage to perceive and relish the five-strand braid woven by her own slim fingers   the five-strand braid grafted to the nape of her neck down she reaches singing out loud   down she reaches for the elastic band bound by her own slim fingers and pulls and pulls until the elastic unwinds   lets loose   the five furling coils of her own dark brown hair

----

Choral journeys through fractures and time to tell
Cora I've been bearing your dreams for you and I've
come to give the dreams back

It's probably true that late at night you shouldn't let the past become a creeping creature that crawls between the layers of your skin and pops out all over, pegging you to your mattress so you can't turn and you can't toss.

But what do you do when you stroke the side of your face in the full-peeled day and remember: this is the skin of my mother. This is the skin of my mother and her sisters and my grandmother and my great-grandmother.

This noisy skin.

At least there was noise.

And tell me, Cora, who were you screeching at anyway? Who were you screeching for? How did you know you had to screech since the day you were born? Was it your breech birth, coming feet-first into the world? Ass-first as you claimed. Ass-first into the world. And who did you think would notice? And who did you think would listen?

In all the noise I learned the power of your will, to survive like rocks and rocks and more rocks and the big flat rock where you built your strength and where you learned to cast rocks. But in all the noise I forgot the pleasure of you. The warmth and breath of you. Your soft body and soft songs, *soft and low just as though*, I could trace the mark again, *a million baby kisses I will deliver if you will only sing that*, fat lines, combs and brushes, *rock-a-bye rock-a-bye your rock-a-bye baby*, across your red-welt skin, your dark hair, the mommy smell of you.

When I stroke the side of my face, I still stroke your eloquence and cry because you are caught in the tangled noise. Laced tight in a bad story and bad dreams and bad songs to sing. You survived but I want more than survival.

I'm getting out. Binding off. Giving your dreams back to you. Balled-up stories now dredged and drawn through. They can't hurt you anymore. They can't hurt me anymore. I'm passing the slipped stitch over, turning the pattern. Casting a loose fit to breathe our loosened beauty.

JOHN McLAUGHLIN

A visual artist and writer, Karen McLaughlin grew up in the Maritimes and after living in diverse regions of Canada now lives in Saltair, a rural area of Vancouver Island, B.C., with her husband John McLaughlin. She was married at eighteen, a mother at twenty-one and committed many years to parenting her two daughters, Sara Juel and Jennifer Morain. In 1987 she began a Visual Arts Major at the University of Regina, then transferred to the Alberta College of Art, from which she graduated with a Major in Painting in 1991. She subsequently continued her studies with creative writing classes at the University of Calgary, and in 1991 had a solo exhibit at the Muttart Art Gallery in Calgary. Feminist theory and literature have profoundly influenced her work.

Press Gang Publishers has been producing vital and provocative books by women since 1975.

A free catalogue is available from Press Gang Publishers, #101 - 225 East 17th Avenue, Vancouver, B.C. V5V 1A6 Canada